MURDER ON LOCATION

A ROSA REED MYSTERY BOOK 4

LEE STRAUSS   DENISE JADEN   NORM STRAUSS

Copyright © 2020 by Lee Strauss

Cover by Steven Novak

Cover Illustration by Amanda Sorenson

All rights reserved.

No part of this book may be reproduced in any form or by any electronic or mechanical means, including information storage and retrieval systems, without written permission from the author, except for the use of brief quotations in a book review.

Library and Archives Canada Cataloguing in Publication Title: Murder on Location : a 1950s cozy historical mystery / Lee Strauss. Names: Strauss, Lee (Novelist), author. Description: Series statement: A Rosa Reed mystery ; 4 Identifiers: Canadiana (print) 20200181327 | Canadiana (ebook) 20200181335 | ISBN 9781774091036 (hardcover) | ISBN 9781774091012 (softcover) | ISBN 9781774091029 (IngramSpark softcover) | ISBN 9781774090992 (EPUB) | ISBN 9781774091005 (Kindle) Classification: LCC PS8637.T739 M95 2020 | DDC C813/.6—dc23

ROSA REED MYSTERIES
IN ORDER

Murder at High Tide
Murder on the Boardwalk
Murder at the Bomb Shelter
Murder on Location
Murder and Rock 'n' Roll
Murder at the Races
Murder at the Dude Ranch
Murder in London
Murder at the Fiesta
Murder at the Weddings

1

One of the first things that attracted Rosa Reed to Dr. Larry Rayburn, assistant medical examiner for the Santa Bonita Police Department, had been that he was the picture of Texas charm. As a former Woman Police Constable for the London Metropolitan Police, Rosa had worked with many pathologists and found most capable and efficient, but they were a little, well, "stiff". Perhaps that came with the job of examining corpses all day. Larry Rayburn, however, defied any stereotypes Rosa had ever had. As a Londoner, she appreciated his gentle formality—but just below that was a funny, unpretentious, and kind man that Rosa enjoyed.

Still, she had to occasionally stifle a giggle when he came to pick her up for a date. He drove a 1948 faded-green Chevrolet pickup truck with its heavy rounded hood, large bug-eyed headlights, and painted grille. Larry had regaled Rosa with stories about the machine, and though he kept saying he meant to trade it in for "a nicer chariot", Rosa suspected her date was a little more attached to the truck than he liked to let on. So tonight, as she watched him trundle into the elegant and expansive Forrester estate in his faithful mechanical steed, she grinned at the incongruous sight.

The Forrester mansion was a sprawling Spanish-style structure, built on a low hill overlooking the Pacific Ocean, and was a testament to her late Uncle Harold's wealth and his success as an oil baron. It boasted many acres of land, manicured gardens, a swimming pool, and a tennis court. The long driveway was lined with swaying palm trees and ended in a circle surrounding an angel-pouring-water fountain.

Not bothering to wait for Larry to come to the door —and saving him from another embarrassing interrogation by her Aunt Louisa who, in Rosa's opinion, was overly enthusiastic about her budding relationship— Rosa stepped out into the warm and breezy California sunshine.

Already out of the truck and opening the passenger door, Larry tipped his straw fedora, winked with his deep-blue eyes twinkling, and said, "Hiya, Miss Reed."

"Hello, Dr. Rayburn," she teased as they were on a first-name basis. Rosa, shifting the crinolines of her black-and-white checkered skirt—embossed with red cherries that matched her red form-fitting, fine-knit sweater—kissed Larry before she climbed into his truck. Gloria, her younger and society-minded cousin, had been with Rosa when they were lingerie shopping and had encouraged the purchase of a bullet brassiere, named such for its rather pointy design. Rosa felt a tad self-conscious wearing it, but Larry, if one could go by his cheeky grin, seemed quite taken with her outfit.

Along with her white half-hat angled on her head of short chestnut curls, short white gloves, and black ballet shoes, Rosa was appropriately dressed for going to the movies and was looking forward to the evening.

Showing at the Santa Bonita Cinema was an action flick called *The Last Clue* starring Nicholas Post. Though Rosa had only recently heard of the star, Gloria had told her, most emphatically, that in America, he was as famous as Cary Grant or Humphrey Bogart.

"You should like this one," Larry said as they moseyed along the main road. "Nicholas Post plays a hard-boiled private investigator."

"I'd hardly call myself hard-boiled." Rosa had recently set up Reed Investigations in Santa Bonita, and though she worked as a private investigator, she didn't think she could be compared to the character in this film.

Larry chuckled and took her hand. "No, darlin', you are definitely of the softer-boiled variety."

"Isn't *The Last Clue* about the mob?"

"Yes, ma'am. Nicholas Post is hired by the mob boss to investigate a string of murders committed by rival gang members."

After arriving at the theater and picking up the reserved tickets, Larry bought two sodas, a big bucket of popcorn to share, and a movie magazine called *Inside the Silver Screen* that featured the very movie they were about to see.

Once seated, Rosa opened the magazine. "East Shore Productions Incorporated produced this film," she said. "It says here they are based in Boston."

"This movie is set there too, isn't it?" Larry said. "In 1912."

"Oh, I didn't realize the year!" Rosa looked closer at the article. "Aunt Louisa was born and raised there," Rosa said, "and though my mother was born in London, she grew up in Boston. She'd have lived there that year. I've never been to Boston, so I think I'm going to enjoy this!"

Larry draped an arm over Rosa's shoulder. "And I'm going to enjoy watching you enjoy it."

The theater darkened and the newsreels began: news that San Francisco's iconic cable line was being replaced by buses, and the winner of the Formula One Drivers' Championship.

"NASCAR is planning an exhibition race here in Santa Bonita," Larry said. "In November."

"Aunt Louisa mentioned that," Rosa returned. "One of her organizations is sponsoring it."

Dramatic music filled the theater as the credits began, and the moviegoers cheered. There was not a seat to spare, and it seemed much of Santa Bonita was excited to start watching.

As the movie progressed, the costumes of the times— the long stiff skirts worn by the women along with their modest long-sleeve blouses with high, button-up collars —intrigued Rosa. And the parasols and big hats could hardly have eased the summer heat. Rosa felt thankful to live in a time where a lady could wear a skirt that ended at the knees, and blouses with no sleeves at all!

But it was the setting of the city of Boston that interested Rosa the most. Boston Harbor differed greatly from Los Angeles on the Pacific Ocean, or London on the River Thames. Her mother had often talked about her transatlantic trip from Boston Harbor to Liverpool. That trip had been significant in several ways. It had been the first time that her mother, Ginger Gold, had met Rosa's father, Basil Reed, another passenger on the ship. It was also the first time Ginger had helped solve a murder with Basil leading the investigation.

Rosa owed her existence to that voyage. Had her mother never gone on that ship, Rosa would never have been born just a few years later. The ship had been called the SS *Rosa*—Rosa's namesake.

Every time the camera panned a shot of the city or the harbor, Rosa, fascinated with it all, leaned forward in her seat. Less impressive to Rosa, however, were the skills of some actors. The main villain in the movie, played by an actor named Scott Huntington, certainly looked the part with his dark, brooding good looks. Still, his acting seemed melodramatic, especially the scene where he was shot, which was a long, painfully dramatic affair causing Rosa to roll her eyes.

The magazine article hinted at a rivalry between this stuntman and Nicholas Post. *Was that actually true or something fabricated for publicity to promote the movie*, Rosa wondered.

"I'd put my money on the dark-haired feller in a real fistfight," Larry whispered in her ear as the two main characters brawled in an Irish pub. "Neither one of 'em seems to know how to operate a gun. They must've shot at each other at least a dozen times in that last scene, and no one got so much as a powder burn."

When the story reached the point where the private investigator rubbed a pencil across an old notepad to reveal hidden letters underneath, Rosa whispered back to Larry, "That's such an overused trick in detective stories. I've never once done that myself, and I doubt if any other detective ever has."

However, Rosa couldn't afford to be critical. Though she'd opened her office a couple of months earlier, business was slow. But she didn't want to think about that problem now and forced herself to focus on the film. Rosa realized that despite her critiques, she was pulled into the movie's plot and felt a sense of disappointment when the story ended.

As they stepped into the evening air and onto the sidewalk along with the rest of the movie patrons, Larry suggested drinks. "There's a bar just down the block."

"Yes, I would like that." Rosa linked her arm with his as they strolled down the street on a pleasantly cool evening.

WHILE IN HER office the next morning, Rosa arranged the magazines on the teak coffee table for the third time. *Did the room look more welcoming now?* She'd placed an ad in the *Santa Bonita Gazette* that had garnered her a few new clients, but not enough to keep her mind and body busy.

She had worked at her mother's office, Lady Gold

Investigations, in London. A long-running establishment—starting its operations since from before Rosa was born—Ginger Gold's business never hurt for clients. Her stellar reputation had been passed by word of mouth and hers was the first agency considered when most people needed a detective.

But how did one gain those qualities with a new business in Santa Bonita, California?

"What are we going to do, Diego?"

Rosa's brown tabby kitten, curled in the corner of the couch, feigned indifference to his owner's plight. He slowly closed his eyes and purred. Apparently, this new office space was even too boring for her cat.

A moment later, the door burst open, and there stood Gloria—all bright eyes and shiny red lipstick.

"Rosa! I thought I might find you here."

Gloria wore an emerald-green A-frame dress patterned with flecks of red and gold. A V-shaped neckline enhanced the capped sleeves. Around the creamy skin of her neck, a pearl choker hung, and her matching pearl belt emphasized her figure. Short curly hair framed her heart-shaped face, and although she'd tested a platinum-blonde look, her natural dark locks suited her much better.

Gloria waved the flyer in her hand. "Look what was posted on the bulletin board."

Rosa picked up on Gloria's infectious smile as she

reached for the paper. *It might be a flyer advertising Reed Investigations*, Rosa thought. However, her name and business were nowhere to be found on the flyer.

"Still a little slow?" Gloria asked, looking around the small office and stating the obvious. But Rosa's rapt attention was now fixed on the small white flyer.

It read: FILMING ON LOCATION IN SANTA BONITA, *QUICK STRIKE*—A WESTERN FILM BY DIRECTOR FREDERICK FORBES. EXTRAS NEEDED!

"That's intriguing," Rosa remarked. "If I'm not mistaken, that's the same director as last night's movie."

"It's the same director," Gloria confirmed. "Frederick Forbes is a very influential figure in that industry."

The qualifications for those who might be interested in extra work were listed under the heading. Prospective extras were people in their twenties with no distinguishing features such as scars or birthmarks on their faces. On the first day of filming, the possible extras had to be prepared to spend the first few hours going through the selection process, and then came makeup and wardrobe allocation.

Gloria came around Rosa and peered over her shoulder to read the flyer, even though Rosa couldn't imagine that her cousin hadn't already memorized every word. "It starts tomorrow," Gloria said. "I already asked if I could miss class—I thought the experience could be helpful." Gloria was a student at a local acting studio. She waved her hands around at the empty office. "It looks as though you're free too. Why don't you come with me?"

The idea of being in a movie—a Frederick Forbes film, no less—pumped more than a little extra adrenaline through Rosa's veins. It certainly beat rearranging coffee-table magazines all day while waiting for the telephone to ring.

"Rosa?" Gloria prodded. "You'll do it with me?"

"I don't know," Rosa hedged. "Acting isn't something I do well." She was purposely modest. In her line of work, she often had to pretend to be someone she wasn't.

Gloria pouted. "You don't have to act as an extra, not really. Anyway, I'll do all the work, you just have to respond to my cues." Gloria tugged on Rosa's arm. "Come on! It'll be fun!"

Rosa's hesitancy had nothing to do with acting, and she knew it. It had everything to do with a certain detective's fiancée, Charlene Winters, who Rosa knew would be on the set.

Rosa sat on the couch beside Diego and sorted out her crinolines and her emotions. Hadn't she carefully filed away her tumultuous romance with Miguel Belmonte into the past? Hadn't she been enjoying the time spent with her new boyfriend, the intelligent and respected Dr. Larry Rayburn, who had the prestigious position of assistant medical examiner?

Hadn't she *moved on*?

Rosa reached over to pet her kitten's soft fur. "What do you think, Diego? Can you live without me for a day?"

Diego's eyelids opened briefly but shut again as if the effort to look up at Rosa was too much. Rosa's mind spun quickly. Just because Charlene Winters would be on set, didn't mean she and Gloria would encounter the actress. Movie sets were notoriously busy places, and she knew she'd be one of many extras who milled about. *And what about Miguel?* Since he had his job to do at the Santa Bonita Police Department, there was no need to worry about him showing up.

Her choice was to while away the time in her office, hoping a client would call, or making her cousin happy.

She smiled up at Gloria. "Let's do it."

2

The drive back to the Forrester mansion was pleasant, except for keeping her hairstyle in place. It was a sacrifice that must be made if she wanted to drive her 1953 Corvette convertible with the top down. Even though it was September, the weather still felt like summer. Accustomed to the drastic change of seasons that happened in her native Britain, Rosa would probably be curled up in front of the fireplace in the sitting room of the perennially chilly, old stone structure of Hartigan House with a cup of tea and a good book if she were there.

Life at the Forrester mansion sometimes felt like a perpetual holiday in the south of France. Many of the world's events were discussed while lounging around the pool. Any one of the Forresters could often be found reading newspapers and magazines as the warm ocean breeze rustled through decorative palm trees.

Diego lay contentedly on the leather seat between Rosa and Gloria as the girls chatted excitedly about the stars of the film—the seasoned award-winning actor Nicholas Post, and the younger, up-and-coming Scott Huntington.

"They were both in the film last night," Rosa said.

Gloria nodded. "I've read that Mr. Forbes thinks they make a good team." Her expression turned dreamy. "Scott Huntington is a real cool cat, but Nicholas Post is an absolute dreamboat. I'm sure they'll both look gorgeous in their costumes." Gloria checked her reflection in the mirror of the sun visor and pushed wayward strands under her headscarf.

"Don't Be Cruel" came on the radio for the hundredth time—one of the most popular songs to be played since its release that summer—and the crooning of the pop-star craze, Elvis Presley, filled the air. Gloria moved her shoulders and sang along.

The song reminded Rosa of the local band, Mick and the Beat Boys. The "Mick" in question was Detective Miguel Belmonte, Rosa's high school crush. They were over now—he was engaged to another—but the song stirred up strong emotions she'd rather forget. She reached for the silver knob on the dashboard and turned the volume down.

"Hey!" Gloria protested.

Rosa drove up the long, palm-tree-lined drive to the Forrester mansion and parked the Corvette in front of the fountain. Clarence had made space for her vehicle in the six-car garage, but with the weather being continually temperate, Rosa didn't mind leaving it at the curb, especially if she planned on using it again soon.

Once they were inside, Gloria announced to all who could hear, "We're going to be in the movies!"

Aunt Louisa called out from the living room. "What are you going on about, Gloria?"

Rosa and Gloria followed the matriarch's voice. Louisa Forrester, half-sister to Rosa's mother, Ginger, had been married to the late Harold Forrester, a self-made millionaire. Sadly, he died during the war, but Aunt Louisa had taken to running the family oil business.

Aunt Louisa was an older-looking version of her daughter, Gloria, with dark hair and blue eyes. She clearly adopted her sense of style from her half-sister, Ginger—Rosa's mother—and looked younger than she was. She sat opposite her mother, Sally Hartigan, on a Scandinavian-style sectional couch. Rosa called the older woman *Grandma Sally*, though technically, she wasn't Rosa's grandmother, but a step-grandmother.

"Rosa and I are going to appear in a movie tomorrow!" Gloria said, ever the optimist.

Aunt Louisa scowled. "What on earth for?"

Used to being challenged in this way, Gloria propped her hand on her hip and stuck her chin in the air. "It'll be fun, Mom, and a good experience for me since I'm going to be a famous actress one day."

"No one looks their best in black and white, dear," Grandma Sally said.

The phenomenon known as *television* had taken over the living rooms of many Americans, and Grandma Sally had grown quite fond of watching it; her eyes darted to Ozzie and Harriet playing in the background.

"There's a new thing in movies called Eastman color, Grandma Sally," Gloria said, shaking her head. "It's less expensive than Technicolor, so more and more films are being shot in color now." Then with a huff, she tugged on Rosa's arm. "Let's sit by the pool."

Rosa hadn't anything pressing to do—the answering service she'd hired would let her know if any calls came into the office—and the invitation to lounge by the pool appealed to her. After delivering Diego to the kitchen where his food and water bowls resided, Rosa skipped upstairs to her room where she changed into a swimming suit, a navy-blue one-piece with white ruffled trim and matching belt.

Slipping into a long fine-knit cover-up and a pair of kitten-heel sandals, Rosa joined Gloria, who'd beaten her poolside. Clarence was there, wearing only swim trunks and a pair of sunglasses. He snapped a newspaper he was reading, folding it in half.

"Elvis Presley is going to be on *The Ed Sullivan Show* this Sunday."

"Ohh." Gloria stared at her brother over pink cat-eye sunglasses. "He's the grooviest! Oh, Rosa, you're going to watch it with me, aren't you?"

"What date is that?" Rosa asked, though she already knew she'd agree. Miguel might be a Mexican version of the pop star, but Rosa couldn't avoid this new sensation. Elvis Presley's face was everywhere.

"September ninth," Clarence recited. "1956."

"Well" Rosa said. "I'm sure the whole country will be watching. I can't very well miss it."

Señora Gomez brought out a pitcher of lemonade. "You get too hot," she said. "Makes you red, like a lobster." Her words were a mild scolding, but her brown eyes smiled as usual.

"Thank you, Señora Gomez," Rosa said. She sipped the cool drink gratefully.

Gloria flipped through the pages of the *Hollywood Secrets* magazine; James Dean on the cover looked debonair.

"Elizabeth Taylor is dating film producer Mike Todd."

Rosa raised a brow. Elizabeth Taylor was younger than Rosa and on her second divorce and third relationship, while Rosa had yet to be married once.

Not that she hadn't come close. She lived in California instead of Britain because of her scandalous fleeing from the altar.

"I dislike the double standard," Clarence said. "People look the other way when their favorite stars get divorced repeatedly, but my friends and colleagues have stopped calling since Vanessa and I split."

"Not fair," Gloria agreed while continuing to browse through the magazine. "But you have to admit, reading about the divorce of Joe DiMaggio and Marilyn Monroe is a bit more exciting."

Clarence lowered his newspaper. "Isn't she on her third marriage now?"

"Yup," Gloria confirmed. "Playwright Arthur Miller.

Señora Gomez returned to the patio. "Telephone for you, Miss Rosa," she said. "It's your nice doctor amigo."

Rosa had worked alongside Larry during various cases, for some of which she'd acted as consultant for the Santa Bonita Police Department. That was how they had met, and the relationship had progressed from there. Rosa wasn't ready for a serious relationship, but she did enjoy his company very much, and couldn't help the smile that spread across her face. After slipping into her cover-up and sandals, she followed the housekeeper into the kitchen. She lifted the receiver, excited to tell Larry about her unconventional plans for the next day.

3

The next morning, Rosa's alarm clock woke her just before five. As it turned out, she hadn't needed the alarm. Even as she stretched her arm to push on the button to stop the bells, Gloria raced into her bedroom.

"Hurry, Rosa! We must get ready!"

It always amazed Rosa how quickly her cousin roused into a state of bright alertness each morning. Rosa liked to cuddle with her kitten for a half hour before she pulled herself out of bed. But her cousin was right; there was no time to relax today. Señora Gomez had promised to cat-sit, and Gloria and Rosa had a film shoot to prepare for.

It was nearly an hour before they were primped and prepared. They made their way down the Forresters' driveway in Rosa's car. The Corvette was a new purchase, and every day Rosa drove the vehicle, she felt a bit more like a movie star, but today, her imagination was a reality—she could end up in a movie!

To preserve their meticulously styled hairdos, they most certainly kept the top up. Rosa gave the engine an extra rev of gas as they sailed onto the Pacific Coast Highway, and Gloria directed her toward Tiendas de Pueblo. They drove mostly in silent anxiety until they reached their destination.

Gloria stiffened. "Oh no."

Rosa glanced over. "What?"

"Look at all the cars! How will we ever find parking? How will we ever get selected?"

Rosa reached over and squeezed Gloria's hand. "If it's meant to be, my dear, it will happen."

And apparently, it was—as Rosa turned a corner onto another street, a vehicle pulled out of a spot along the curb. Rosa quickly clicked on her signal light, and moments later, her Corvette Roadster occupied the space.

As soon as the ignition was off, Rosa and Gloria hopped out of the car and walked toward the Spanish village shops. Long red and white trucks and trailers were parked at the far end of the village, and all along the shopping area, scruffy men in black moved about—carrying furniture and hanging new signage over the current store signs. One man stood on a ladder painting the outside wall of a brightly colored Spanish restaurant.

Rosa and Gloria made their way down the busy street.

Surely someone who is busily preparing the set would know where we're supposed to go, Rosa thought.

In her bubbly voice, Gloria called out to the first crew member they came across. "Excuse me? Do you know where the extras should go for selection?" In case it would help, Gloria held out the flyer she'd been clutching all morning.

The man—barely more than a boy now that Rosa saw him up close—looked up from where he was nailing a new sign for a dress shop. The young man pointed to the far end of the village street where the large trucks were parked. "They're lining up at the wardrobe truck. Keep going to the end, ma'am."

Large white tents had been erected in every nook and cranny. Rosa noted that the sidewalks and street corners were occupied by busy crew members, who moved so briskly, they almost looked as if the workers were running late. They busily prepared bulky film cameras, lighting trees, boom microphones on extendable poles, and many stepladders.

Turning a corner, Rosa and Gloria were greeted by a long line of people that snaked away from one of the trucks.

Gloria sucked in a breath. "There must be a hundred of them already!"

Rosa and Gloria had planned to be there a good half hour before the time marked on the flyer, to get a feel for how it all worked, but they were not the only early arrivals. They tacked themselves onto the end of the line.

Rosa surveyed the fashions of those in front of them. Many were dressed in black and white clothes, but a splattering of bright colors stood out as well.

Gloria whispered to Rosa, "I think we have a good chance."

A wooden ramp angled from the back opening of the large wardrobe. There was more clothing than Rosa had ever seen in one place before—and she had helped run her mother's Regent Street dress shop in London.

Crammed into the truck's trailer, the clothing hung along bars lining the full length. The prospective extras in the line didn't enter the trailer—there wasn't much room between the hanging clothes to do so—but two female crew members, dressed in black, stood on ladders within the trailer. They sorted through the upper rungs of clothing as though they were searching for something specific.

As the line moved forward, Rosa caught glimpses of

two more female wardrobe crew members and one man, maybe in his mid-thirties. The man was probably the oldest crew member she'd set eyes on so far, and as she looked ahead in the line, she also noticed many youthful folks among the numbers. At twenty-eight, Rosa hoped she wasn't too old. Gloria was nearly ten years younger and seemed a better fit for the demographic group.

Two crew members sat at a table. As each person approached, a nod or a shake of the head told them their fate.

Rosa's worry grew as the two men continued to shake their heads, sending hopefuls away. The line held about eighty percent women, and the competition was stiff.

A young lady in her early twenties, stout but not altogether unattractive with nicely done hair and pleasant features, smiled with excitement. She inched forward with the rest of the line, and when she reached the front, was given a white slip of paper. As she turned around to the people behind her, she waved the paper, her joy written on her face. Rosa assumed this meant she had been chosen.

By the time Rosa and Gloria moved within hearing distance of the wardrobe personnel, Rosa had both sets of her fingers crossed behind her back. There was still one man and three brightly dressed women lined up in front of her and Gloria, so Rosa could already guess how this would go.

But before the line moved forward again, a wardrobe crew member, with a men's western-style shirt, vest, and dungarees draped over one arm, rushed up to the two in charge of the selection process. Her hair was red and in messy curls that made her look like she'd already worked a long day, even though it wasn't yet seven in the morning. She shook her head and spoke before she'd made it to her coworkers.

"Mr. Post doesn't like the fit of his costume, and now, he says the shoes don't fit and that we must have ordered the wrong size!" She threw down the leather ensemble on the ramp. "He went mad again and called me incompetent. We have to find a way to fix this!"

The two other wardrobe women asked quick questions such as, "Too big or too small?" and "What's open at this hour?"

One of them waved a frustrated hand at the line of aspiring extras. "We don't have time for this!"

The older man nodded and seemed to stay calmer than the others about the situation. "You ladies deal with the shoes. I'll finish up here."

"Here" clearly meant the selection process of the extras, because seconds later, the three wardrobe women skittered into the trailer and appeared to converse with the other two assistants frantically.

Now, the line had doubled; however, this gentleman seemed much more in control of the selection process. Seconds later, he marched down the side of the line and pointed at people.

"You," he said to the man in front of them in line, this one wearing a navy cardigan and tan slacks. "Head on over to the hair and makeup tent." He handed him a paper and added, "Here is your voucher for the day."

To the ladies, he said, "Thanks for coming. We won't be needing you today."

He took no time for pleasantries and simply moved down the line to Rosa and Gloria. He opened his mouth like he was about to repeat the words already on his tongue, but then he stopped in place and looked at them from head to toe. Seconds later, he was pulling two papers from his stack and handing them over. Rosa's heart rate skittered.

"You'll find hair and makeup in that tent," he said, already moving on to the next in line, "and don't forget to fill in your voucher for the day so that you can get paid."

Rosa and Gloria quickly moved out of line and tried to keep their grins subdued until they got out of eyeshot of the others.

"We get paid for this?" Rosa murmured on their way to the tent.

Gloria bit her lip. "Apparently so."

4

On the far side of the hair and makeup tent, a smaller line snaked from the entrance. This one was predominantly made up of men, crouched down filling in their vouchers, using a knee as a table. Rosa reached for a pen in her purse. Since there was nowhere to sit and write, Rosa and Gloria used each other's backs as tables to fill in their names, addresses, and phone numbers. Rosa read over the long section of fine print on the back of her voucher before signing it. It had a lot of fancy wording, but was basically a simple day contract, releasing the film production company to use their image and ensuring that if they stayed until they were dismissed, they would be paid for their time.

This process helped pass the wait, and by the time they were done, they were inside the flap of the tent. At least ten chairs were lined up, all filled with extras.

Several were having their hair styled, and others were having makeup applied—even the men.

As though they were thinking the same thing, the next man to take a seat asked, "Do the men have to wear makeup?"

The makeup lady in charge of fixing him up said, "Yes, I'm afraid that in a color film like this one if you don't wear it, your face will look like a ghost."

The man didn't argue after that, but as Rosa took the empty chair beside him, the two makeup artists were well into a conversation of their own.

"Pam said he refused to have an ounce of their makeup applied. He brought his own, which was not the right kind for daylight. She had to get Mr. Forbes to talk to him in the key makeup trailer."

"Honestly, I don't understand these movie stars sometimes," Rosa's makeup lady remarked.

"Most are okay, but this one . . . pfft." The other lady shook her head.

As they chattered on with their gossip, Rosa listened in. She tried to hear who this difficult star might be. When the makeup artist absentmindedly dabbed makeup to Rosa's face, though, Rosa said, "Oh! I already applied makeup this morning. Is it not enough?"

The makeup artist shook her head. "We have special selections that work best for film." Rosa figured this lady knew what she was talking about and let her do her job, which started with removing Rosa's own makeup. Having someone else apply makeup had the bonus of making her feel like the celebrity of the day. When the makeup lady applied false eyelashes, Rosa admitted to herself that the effect wasn't bad.

Soon she moved over to a hairdresser's chair, but she was out of it almost as soon as she was in it. She was marked as "Approved" and sent toward the extras' holding area after an explanation she would probably wear a wig. She was told the extras' holding area was a roped-off zone on the far side of the tent, but Rosa waited until Gloria was also through with makeup and hairstyling before moving to the next stage of this conveyor belt of a business.

Gloria was all giddy smiles by the time she got up from the hairdresser's chair and joined Rosa near the tent opening. "I feel like such a movie star," she gushed.

Rosa regarded her younger cousin. They'd given her a blonde wig in the style that reminded Rosa of many saloon girls she had seen in other westerns, with big sausage curls pinned in a half-up style. This film was set in the year 1875, and so her wig seemed very fitting.

"Very nice!" Rosa said.

Down the street, the extras' holding position had a

rope around a sizable area and at least a hundred folding wooden chairs within it. Half the chairs were already occupied. Some people sat in rows, but many had been moved into groups of extras who already knew each other and wanted to sit together.

As Rosa and Gloria walked in that direction, they passed another large white trailer. On its door, the sign read, "Hair and Makeup". A block of stairs pushed up to the side door, and just as Rosa wondered if this was where the actual movie stars went to get ready, the door swung open, and one walked down the stairs.

He wore a black leather jacket and jeans, was of medium build, and had dark hair. But it was difficult to see his face properly because he kept his chin down. He crossed the parking lot and headed toward a trailer with a star on its door.

Gloria grabbed Rosa's arm so sharply it almost made her yelp in surprise. "Oh heavens, Rosa! That's Scott Huntington!"

The actor turned his head subtly at the recognition. Rosa could see his dark, brooding eyes, which she remembered from *The Last Clue*. A handsome man, yes, but his angry scowl compromised his attractiveness as he marched toward his trailer. Before he arrived there, however, another voice called out, "Mr. Huntington? They're ready for you on set."

Without raising his head, Scott Huntington angled right and followed the man who had called for him.

"Not the friendliest fellow, is he?" Rosa said as soon as he was out of earshot.

Gloria shushed her. "He does his own stunts which makes him unpopular with both regular stuntmen who think he's stealing their jobs and other actors who feel like they don't measure up if they don't do their own stunts. I read about him in *Modern Screen*."

Once Mr. Huntington was out of sight, there was nothing left to do but wait.

"Let's go see who else is here," Gloria said, excitement brimming in her every word. She tugged Rosa's hand toward the other trailers, but Rosa hesitated.

"Maybe we should do as we were told." Rosa could just imagine being sent home before they even made it onto the set of the movie.

Gloria dismissed Rosa's concerns with a wave of a hand. "Nobody will know. Besides, look at the long line at the extras' holding area. There's no rush."

Rosa supposed that if they were caught hanging around where they shouldn't be, they could simply say they were lost. With all the trailers and tents, it would be easy to get disoriented on the lot.

The round-cornered silver trailers formed a semicircle. All the other doors with stars faced the middle. Rosa held back Gloria with her arm as they approached the inner circle. Three actors milled in the space—a man and two women. One of the blonde women stood off to one side with a script in her hands, clearly practicing her lines. When she turned and looked up, recognition struck Rosa, and a shiver of nerves shot down her spine. It was Miguel's fiancée, Charlene Winters.

Rosa had spent her teen years in Santa Bonita, waiting for the end of the Second World War. When she met Private Belmonte, she fell in love. Perhaps it was the intensity of the times or the passion of an emotional young girl, but Rosa had never felt so deeply for a man as she had for Miguel. Meeting up with him again after eleven years—and one broken engagement later—had been a shock to Rosa's system. Even though sparks between them were hard to ignore, Miguel had moved on with Charlene, and Rosa had stepped out with Larry.

Charlene was a beautiful lady who looked like the movie star she aimed to be. Her hair was in a fancy updo, and she had visited the makeup trailer as her face looked gorgeous, although, like Rosa's and Gloria's, exaggerated.

Rosa tugged Gloria behind one of the trailers and out of sight.

"Ow, Rosa! What the heck?"

"It's Charlene Winters," Rosa whispered.

Gloria's eyes widened. "Detective Belmonte's fiancée, right? She looks even prettier than in the commercials."

Rosa forced her eyes off Charlene to the actor she was with. Rosa recognized the striking man with his sandy hair and bright-blue eyes from the last movie she'd seen with Larry. Nicholas Post was a sight to behold, even more good-looking in real life. It was hard to ignore his flirting with Charlene, who, Rosa noticed, wore slippers and a robe. Rosa suspected she had yet to visit the wardrobe trailer. The way Mr. Post leaned into her and caused her to throw her head back and laugh every few seconds suggested his words were filled with apple butter.

Charlene suddenly called out, "Leave him be!" As though she was trying to deliver her lines with full emotion, she stretched out a hand. Her words were loud enough. But there was something unconvincing about them, especially when she added, "It's too dangerous!"

Rosa and Gloria shuffled closer to hear better. The spectacle was fascinating.

"Better," Mr. Post said to her. "But when you deliver a dramatic line like this one, you want to say it like you're shooting the other actor right in the heart with it." Charlene nodded, and Mr. Post backed up a few feet and said, "Try again."

Someone moved behind Rosa and Gloria, and they didn't realize what was happening until the lady was speaking. "Miss Winters? They're ready for you in wardrobe."

The warmth of humiliation crept up her neck as Rosa ducked when Charlene turned to the voice. *Dear heavens, did Charlene Winters see me?*

"Extras' holding is back that way," the lady in the white smock told them, a clip to her voice. Rosa held up a hand of apology as they backed away, returning to the extras' holding area.

"How embarrassing!" Gloria exclaimed once they were out of earshot. Still, she didn't know the half of it —Gloria was unaware of Rosa's wartime romance with Miguel Belmonte and that Miguel's fiancée had just seen her sneaking around where she didn't belong.

5

A friendly middle-aged man with a receding hairline approached Rosa and Gloria as they waited with the other extras. "Hi! I'm Bernie. First time, I hear?"

Rosa figured there was no point in hiding their inexperience. "Yes. You too?"

He let out a loud laugh as he followed them to a small bank of open chairs. "No, no. I've been doing this for years."

"In Santa Bonita?" Gloria asked, doubt etched on her face.

"Nah, mostly at the studios. In Hollywood."

"Really?" Gloria's smile was a real charmer, although her eyes held a million questions.

But it seemed Bernie was done being their personal welcoming committee. He pointed to a circle of chairs in the corner. "If you like to knit, there's a knitting circle over there."

Rosa wrinkled her nose, more in confusion than in distaste for knitting, but Bernie took it as the latter and said, "Or if cards are your thing, there's always a couple of good games going on." He motioned to people playing cards. "There's a chess game going on over that way."

Rosa was dubious. Weren't they here to act in a movie?

Bernie added, "The only place you can't sit is over there." He motioned to a group of men and one woman close to the rope and as far away from the others as possible. They all gestured expressively with their hands, though Rosa couldn't quite hear what they were saying. "Those are the 'stunties'. They keep to themselves."

With that, Bernie left Rosa and Gloria and headed over to a nearby card game. A couple of folks sat reading books, but most people here seemed to know each other. Rosa wondered how many regularly worked as extras in the Hollywood studios.

A short time later, the man from behind the folding table stood and yelled, "Can I have everyone's attention, please!" The din of chatter quieted. "For those of you who don't know me, I'm John Salvatore, the AD on this production."

Gloria leaned in and whispered to Rosa. "That stands for assistant director."

John Salvatore looked around the tent as he continued. "Don't speak to the director, and don't speak to any of the actors. It's looking like a long day. They've already started on an action scene, but once they're done, we have several bits to shoot within the town square. It's an action film, so if we select you to go to set, be aware of your exact positioning so no one gets hurt. Most of you can expect to be here sitting in holding for a good portion of the next twelve hours."

Twelve hours?

All that waiting around, and it sounded as though they might not even make it into the movie! With no further pleasantries, John Salvatore nodded then rushed out of the roped-off area. Rosa and Gloria looked at each other. It explained why the stunt actor, Scott Huntington, had been so closed off. He must have regularly been bothered by disobedient extras or roaming fans. Plus, Rosa recalled the discussion she had overheard in the makeup tent about a difficult actor. Mr. Huntington had just come from the makeup trailer, so as much as he hadn't wanted his makeup done, it had likely been forced on him by the director.

"I guess those in the know had a good idea to bring a deck of cards," Rosa said. She sighed, sat back into her seat, and accepted she might have closed her office to sit outside wasting time all day. And here she'd thought she was getting away from her boredom! She opened her handbag, sure that at some point, she'd stuffed a paperback inside. Her fingers reached the book, and she smiled as she recollected the title: *Minority Report* by Philip K. Dick. The story—a police commissioner ran a program involving mutants who could see crimes before they were committed—intrigued Rosa, who was now halfway through the book and hooked.

"You brought a book?" Gloria said. "You can't read! I need you to keep me company."

Rosa chuckled. "This is your chance to get to know a few seasoned veterans. Perhaps you should join Bernie at the card table."

Gloria huffed. "Maybe I will." She pushed back her chair and bumped into a young man, causing him to spill his coffee. "Oh, excuse me."

He held his cup away from his body, looked down at his shirt, and made sure he hadn't soiled it.

"No problem," he said. "I don't think I got any on me." He smiled at her and then kind of froze in place.

Gloria stared back for a moment, and Rosa couldn't help but notice the interaction.

The lanky man had curly hair, soft brown eyes, and full, expressive lips. "Are you famous?" he asked, his eyes widening.

Gloria giggled, her hand flying to cover her mouth, then answered coyly, "Maybe."

"Oh, you kind of look like you might be," the man said.

"Why, thank you." Gloria smiled back sweetly. "I will take that as a compliment."

Rosa pretended to read but watched her flirty cousin over her book's edge. Gloria had a way with the opposite sex.

The man extended his long arm. "My name is Ben . . . Ben Applebaum." He shook Gloria's hand, and she made a cute little curtsy and batted her eyelashes.

Rosa rolled her eyes.

"I'm Gloria Forrester."

"It's a pleasure to meet you, Miss Forrester."

"Likewise."

Rosa stared with no pretense of reading.

Gloria must've sensed her pointed gaze. "Oh," she said as if she had only just remembered that she hadn't come to the movie set alone. "This is my cousin Rosa Reed."

"Very pleased to meet you, Miss Reed. I, uh . . ."

Mr. Applebaum was interrupted by Mr. Salvatore, who rushed into the area. An older man with slicked-back gray hair and thick black glasses followed the AD. He wore suspenders over a cardigan, but his giant gray mustache was his most striking feature.

Gloria whispered to Rosa. "That's Frederick Forbes."

For such a big name in the movie industry, Rosa thought it odd for him to be standing in the extras' holding area, especially since they had just been instructed not to speak to him. Ever.

Many extras watched Mr. Forbes and Mr. Salvatore as they conversed in hushed tones near the rope opening. Mr. Forbes motioned to the stuntie group, then pointed at Rosa and Gloria. Without saying a word to the extras, the director turned and marched away. Mr. Salvatore wandered through the holding area, touching people on the shoulder, and murmuring to them.

Reaching Rosa, Gloria, and Ben Applebaum, he tapped Gloria and Rosa on their shoulders and said, "Go to set," and then, as if he knew they would need additional instruction, he added, "Just stay with the others; I'll place you when I get there."

Rosa assumed "set" was the area they had walked through earlier that morning, where the crew had been busily painting and posting wooden facades and boardwalks.

Ben Applebaum gave a little wave, "I guess I'll see ya around."

Gloria waved back and smiled. "Bye."

"He's kinda cute, isn't he?" Gloria said as they

walked back toward the set.

Rosa remained noncommittal. "There are a lot of good-looking men around here."

When they reached the set, they found a small group of extras hovering about, awaiting instruction. Crew members moving tables and chairs rushed by as others still stood propped on ladders, decorating. Two struggled with a large sign that read SALOON.

They were ushered into the wardrobe, where Rosa and Gloria, having been designated "saloon girls" were assigned costumes.

Rosa needed Gloria's assistance to get into the tight whale-bone bodice, black lace over red, with a very low-cut lace-trimmed neckline that exposed rather a lot of cleavage.

As her mother would say, *Oh mercy*. Rosa had never seen her bosom in such a display.

"Ooh la la," Gloria said, laughing aloud.

Gloria's costume wasn't any less revealing, and both dresses ended at the knee. Thankfully they were given black stockings.

Rosa whispered to Gloria as she tugged up on the lace trim of her neckline. "I feel exposed."

"Don't be silly." Gloria twirled in front of the mirror. "Real actresses have to wear far less sometimes."

Other extras now dressed in costume milled about.

Men wore leather chaps and vests with cowboy hats and boots, or were dressed in the pinstriped suits and top hats of the business class. Ladies flitted like hummingbirds—their long flowing dresses in soft pastels and large-brimmed hats adorned with grand feathers. All were gossiping about people on the set. The name Scott Huntington came up more than once, except now it wasn't spoken with quite the same awe as Gloria had uttered it. Grumblings of "overacting" and "difficult to work with" painted a clear picture of what these people thought of the bristly stunt actor.

Regardless, Rosa would only be here for one day, and she could certainly handle one annoying personality. Besides, she was more excited to see the famed Nicholas Post in action.

Time ticked by, and Rosa checked the clock overhead often. The day had started early and dragged on. Rosa's initial anticipation had seeped out a few hours earlier. She half wished they hadn't been selected so she could still be sitting in her chair in the holding area reading her book, or better yet, been sent home. For Gloria's sake, she hoped for a turn in fortunes.

Eventually, John Salvatore made his way to set and directed the extras to the spots where they should stand. When he came to Rosa and Gloria, he pushed them toward the saloon. "Stand on the boardwalk. Look sensual."

Rosa wasn't sure how she could look more sensual without stripping down to nothing.

Mr. Salvatore yelled, "Quiet on the set!" so loudly, it scared her into standing up straight. The group of stunties arrived, and the mustached director placed them throughout the street, giving them specific directions: some would run, one would jump back, one would fall to the ground. Apparently, this would all happen on the cue of an upcoming gunshot.

Rosa and Gloria looked at each other with exuberant grins. This would be quite a thrilling chase scene!

Frederick Forbes called out, "Let's rehearse with our cast," and then, as though no one would have heard the loud director, Mr. Salvatore repeated in an even louder voice, "Rehearsal with our cast!"

John Salvatore rushed toward the stars dressing rooms. Another seemingly endless amount of time passed while the set decorations were adjusted, and the extras were moved to their "first marks". Eventually, the ladders were cleared out of the way.

The cast members appeared. Rosa caught her breath when she first saw Charlene. She looked sophisticated in a pale-blue satin dress, narrow at the waist with layered skirts and a massive bustle at the back. Her blonde hair was partially covered by a big floppy hat, which shaded her attractive face.

Mr. Forbes made his way straight over to her. "We won't see you on this one, sweetheart," he said. "But you can say your line on *Action*, and we'll keep you there for Nick's eye line. All right?"

Next to arrive was Scott Huntington, which immediately created some murmuring among the extras and crew. He wore a cowboy hat, leather chaps and western boots, along with a scowl. He headed for an upper balcony near the side of the street where Rosa and Gloria leaned against the saloon railing. Grabbing a balcony post, he pulled himself up with ease.

Mr. Forbes called to him. "Scott, this is just a rehearsal. No need to add all your stunts along the way. Just give us a path."

Mr. Huntington glared back.

Mr. Forbes added, "Start down here for now," as though he hadn't been clear enough. "And no blood pack during rehearsal. We'll save the clothes for shooting."

The crew stilled, waiting for a reaction between the stunt actor and the director. When no outburst followed, they relaxed and continued on with their duties.

Rosa wondered what it would be like to work on a movie set every day where tensions between people often ran high.

6

Nicholas Post arrived dressed as a cowboy with a gun belt and holster. His entourage included a redheaded woman dressed in a simple blue dress cinched at the waist with a matching belt, holding a clipboard and pen, and taking notes as she walked. Members of the hair and makeup crew fussed over Mr. Post, and Rosa heard one of them refer to the redheaded woman as Miss Williamson.

"Nicholas, if you don't mind taking your mark." The director pointed to a painted X on the ground. To Charlene, he said, "Ready, Miss Winters?"

When she nodded, the director shouted, "Rehearsal with the cast."

Mr. Salvatore promptly repeated the direction.

Mr. Post called out, "Shouldn't I rehearse with the gun?"

Mr. Forbes yelled into a megaphone. "Dennis from props! We need the gun on set!"

Rosa found the whole process, if unorganized, fascinating. All the magic of a finished film was a long list of slow-moving exercises.

After another long wait, a young crew member in what appeared to be long swim trunks, a white t-shirt, and sporting shoulder-length, sun-bleached hair, ran in from the direction of the production trucks. When he reached Mr. Post, he held out the gun, opened the barrel to it, and gave instructions on its use, though Mr. Post looked too busy surveying the street in front of him to be paying attention. He snatched the gun, clicked the barrel back into place, and turned away, effectively dismissing the props attendant.

John Salvatore made an announcement. "Ladies and gentlemen, we have a gun on set. This revolver is filled with blanks. It is not a danger to anybody, but it will make a loud noise. We're looking for natural reactions to the blast, and we want a lot of scattering when it happens. Just be aware not to get in the way of our actors."

After that, extras were told to go to their first marks, and crew members were instructed to clear. Mr. Salvatore shouted, "Background action."

Instantly, the shopping village in front came to life. Extras walked down the street, pretending to talk but not making a sound. Some stood at shops as if bartering with shop owners. As instructed, Rosa leaned on a post that the railing was attached to and tried to look sensual. In reality, she felt ridiculous. Gloria pouted her lips, looking far more believable, though still outlandish. Rosa made sure not to catch Gloria's eye. They would no doubt ruin the scene if they both burst out laughing.

Frederick Forbes called, "Action!"

Charlene said her line, "Sheriff Jennings, don't do it." Her voice was quiet, and the effect of the line less dramatic than when she'd rehearsed it with Mr. Post earlier near the trailers.

"What?" Mr. Post shouted. "I can't hear her."

Charlene recited her line again, "Sherriff Jennings, don't do it!" this time so loud that the neighboring town could likely hear it. The moment was awkward, and Rosa didn't envy Charlene, whose face had gone beet-red.

Mr. Huntington, in position on the balcony, used one hand to swing over the rail—nearly knocking into two female extras. They both let out a surprised shriek as their parcels went flying, but Mr. Huntington paid them no attention and zigzagged through the make-believe town. He banged into boardwalk signs, pushed people out of his way, and jumped over more railings. He did it all so fluidly; it looked as though it had been rehearsed with the extras and set decorations a hundred times.

A loud gunshot rang out into the air. Rosa had heard gunshots before, but the set was so quiet at that moment, that the loud sound made her jump. She froze for about two seconds, looked to Gloria, and then hitched her skirt as she scooted back to the saloon swinging doors.

A bloodstain bloomed on the shoulder of Mr. Huntington's canvas shirt, and if one hadn't known better, one could have been forgiven for thinking the actor had been shot. He let out a loud moan, stumbled a few feet, dropped to his knees, and then let out a sharp gasp. Rosa could recognize it as acting—perhaps even the overacting he'd been accused of—and she recalled mention of a blood pack he had been instructed not to pop.

"Cut on rehearsal!"

As Mr. Forbes approached the actors, Mr. Post's eyes darkened in anger. "I can't chase him if he's here making a spectacle in the street! He was just supposed to pause for one second and then move on, right?"

Scott Huntington wore a scowl as the two other men talked about him.

"Yes, yes. Don't worry, Nick," Mr. Forbes said, his voice rich with aggravation. "We'll fix it. We'll start you farther back and—"

"So now I have to run farther?"

"Don't worry; we'll fix it." Mr. Forbes turned to the crew. "Reset!"

Mr. Salvatore repeated the same instruction. Rosa wondered if that was his job, to repeat anything that the director said.

Mr. Forbes patted Mr. Post on the shoulder as he guided him back to his marked X. He spoke to Mr. Huntington with forced calm. "I guess you didn't hear me, Scott. Let's leave the blood packs and the knocking around of set pieces for the real thing, alright?"

Mr. Forbes made his way through the street, giving specific directions to several of the stunties. To Rosa's surprise, the director strolled right up to them. "Let's get these extras out of here." Rosa felt a bloom of disappointment. This was just getting interesting! But then the director added, pointing at Rosa and Gloria, "Keep the saloon girls. Move them closer to the gunshot. I liked their reactions."

Rosa was more than a little surprised when John Salvatore placed her and Gloria almost right between the X from where Nicholas Post would be shooting, and the other X where Scott Huntington would react after being shot.

"Make sure to stay to the right of the Xs," the assistant director said, "or you'll throw everything off and get in the gunshot's way."

Rosa shared a look with Gloria. They didn't have to be told that twice.

It took a few minutes for crew members to clean and reassemble all the elements of the set that Scott Huntington had bowled over. Mr. Forbes then called for rehearsal again.

As the other extras mimed, walked, and shopped around them, Rosa and Gloria feigned a disinterested discussion. Mr. Forbes called out, "Action," and Bernie wandered across the street to mime with them.

A risky move, Rosa thought. *Walking across the street while the chase was clearly in motion.*

Scott Huntington again pushed through crowds and knocked over signs as Mr. Post took his shot. Shockingly, Mr. Huntington popped another blood pack. This time, when he crouched as if in pain, Mr. Forbes left him there for a second or two, before calling out on the megaphone, "Go, Scott! Run!"

Mr. Huntington stood and ran, but again, Mr. Post was so close he could easily catch the man.

When Mr. Forbes called, "Cut," Mr. Post started to rage. Throwing his hands into the air, he said, "This isn't working! He stayed there way too long. I could easily have caught him, for crying out loud. We don't have time for his melodramatics. We need a different plan here!"

Patiently hearing out his lead actor's complaints,

the director nodded. "Okay, we'll reset. Why don't you take a break? In the meantime, let me deal with Scott and figure this out."

"Are you also going to figure out the overripe acting?" Mr. Post bellowed. "You assured me I wouldn't be associated with poor acting on this one. I wouldn't think you'd want your name dragged through the mud either."

The director's face puffed with reined-in impatience. "I'll figure it out, Nick."

Mr. Post let out an even louder huff then stormed toward the trailers.

Mr. Forbes called out to his assistant director, "Send everyone on a relax, John. We need to reset everything."

Gloria grabbed Rosa's arm to pull her toward the holding area, but Rosa resisted for a second. Her curiosity was stirred, and she wasn't in a hurry to leave just yet. Instead, she said, "I actually want to find a restroom."

Bernie, overhearing, pointed. "There's a honey wagon over by my assistant's trailer."

It took Rosa a second to realize he was talking to her. "A honey wagon?"

He grinned. "A restroom. If you ask John Salvatore, he'll tell you to use the outhouses, but believe me, the honey wagon is much nicer. You'll see it marked if you go past all the trailers to the end."

Rosa nodded and let Gloria and Bernie go off in the other direction. By this time, crew members rushed around set, trying to put together everything that Mr. Huntington had pulled apart. Rosa had seen these same crew members working hard this morning trying to get everything meticulously in place, so it was unsurprising to see the frustration on their faces.

One of the wardrobe ladies from outside the truck earlier stood near Mr. Forbes and Scott Huntington, looking like she was itching to become part of the conversation.

When Mr. Forbes finally acknowledged her, she talked in a loud, frustrated burst of words. "We need his shirt right away! I have no idea how we're going to get the blood out. I thought you said you were saving the blood for the last take. We weren't expecting this during rehearsal."

Mr. Forbes didn't rattle easily. He simply nodded and angled both toward the wardrobe truck. The honey wagon was in the same direction, so Rosa trailed at a distance.

The wardrobe lady was clearly in a hurry. She kept moving ahead of the two men and then turned back, hoping they would speed up. Rosa heard another crew member grumble, "At this rate, we're going to be here all night!"

As Rosa was about to move on, a star-marked door swung open, and Mr. Post skipped down the stairs, a bright smile on his face. Interested in what a movie star's trailer might look like, she peered a little closer, but Mr. Post threw the door shut behind him before she could even get a tiny glimpse.

As though out of nowhere, his female assistant appeared and passed him a piece of tissue. She also held a bakery bag and a coffee cup. After she motioned to his face, Mr. Post used the tissue across a streak of what looked like bright-pink lipstick.

Rosa felt her eyes widen at being privy to something so secretive in a movie star's life. This was the sort of thing you would read in those tabloid magazines —where reporters dedicated their lives to getting one secret photograph of a movie star's latest tryst.

But she had stayed too long because, at that second, Mr. Post turned her way and spotted her. His smile grew as if he was not embarrassed at being caught in a secretive rendezvous. But that wasn't the worst of it. Rosa gasped when the figure of Charlene Winters, a small smile playing on her lips, emerged from the door of the trailer.

7

John Salvatore rushed back to his table and called for everyone's attention. "Those who were already on set, we're going back. Right now! Mr. Forbes is not in a good mood, so I suggest you keep your mouths shut and just do your job."

Rosa grimaced. "This doesn't sound like quite as much fun now, does it?"

"This is ordinary movie business excitement," Gloria said with a dismissive wave of her hand. "Drama on and off set. It's what makes it so tantalizing."

They went directly to their first marks and stood there. Time passed. All the while, Rosa's mind spun. What she had just seen made it hard to concentrate. The set had not been restored to order—ladders were being moved around, chairs were being nailed back together, and more than once, Rosa and Gloria had to move out of the way for crew members to work. Many let out quiet, frustrated oaths under their breath.

Rosa noticed several men standing around with notepads and cameras. She assumed that the press had now shown up for the shooting.

"We're already two hours behind!" Mr. Forbes yelled, obviously finished with pretending he was calm and collected. "That's not how that horse trough was positioned! Can't anyone do anything right around here?" Blustering at John Salvatore, he said, "Did you check with wardrobe? How are they doing with those bloodstains?"

"They got most of it out, Mr. Forbes, but it's taking some time to dry."

"It doesn't have to be dry," the director barked in return. "It just has to look dry. Come on! Time is money." He marched off behind the cameras, and Rosa assumed it was to ensure everything was ready on the technical end of things.

"Let's get the cast on set," Mr. Salvatore shouted. "I want to be ready to shoot the second they have that shirt!"

Looking more confident since the break, Charlene returned to set, and Rosa wondered how many hundreds of times she had practiced her one line. For the first time, their eyes met. Charlene's pretty face morphed from surprise at seeing Rosa to displeasure.

Rosa smiled wanly then glanced away. There was no reason she should feel embarrassed. It wasn't like she was stalking Charlene, though Rosa didn't doubt Charlene would present the story to Miguel that way.

So what? She didn't care what Miguel Belmonte thought of her anymore. She didn't. Besides, she had Larry now. She imagined how he'd laugh, his voice warm and buttery, when she'd tell him this story later.

Nicholas Post's arrival rescued Rosa from her reverie. He joked around with the cameramen, and the hair and makeup ladies who came to touch up his face. His previous demonstration of frustration was gone—*no doubt his little tryst in the leading lady's trailer helped with that*—and his light and jovial presence seemed to put the rest of the cast and crew at ease.

The last to arrive, Scott Huntington strutted onto the set, wearing a crisp new canvas shirt.

"It's our only spare," the brunette from wardrobe said.

"We'll get it in one shot," Mr. Forbes returned. "We have to."

Mr. Huntington pulled himself up onto the balcony.

"We'll have to shoot this one," Mr. Forbes yelled loudly so that everyone could hear. "We're just too far behind." Then to Mr. Huntington, "I liked the jump onto the table. And the zigzaggin' worked. We have our stunties in place now, so take the same path as you did during rehearsal, they're the ones you should knock into."

Rosa thought it strange that Mr. Forbes, this commanding and well-known director, was letting a stunt actor run the show, but perhaps he didn't have a choice. He needed this actor for his strong stunt work, even if his acting ability wasn't stellar. Seeing everything Mr. Forbes had to manage, and for only one small scene, gave Rosa a whole new respect for directors.

Mr. Forbes called for "final touches", to which a dozen hair, makeup, and wardrobe ladies rushed onto the set and touched up the cast members and even a few extras. One hairdresser came to tidy Rosa and Gloria's hair, spraying them both with stiff hairspray.

Crew members and ladders were cleared, and as the last of the makeup assistants moved out of the way, a hush came over the set. Nervous energy filled the air.

"Are we ready to roll the camera?" Mr. Forbes yelled.

"Oh, wait!" Nicholas Post said. "I left the prop gun in my dressing room."

Mr. Forbes took an obvious calming breath before he opened his mouth to yell, "Dennis, props? We need the gun from Mr. Post's dressing room!"

Everyone stood still. The stars' dressing rooms were out of view, a good walk away, and Rosa could only imagine how frustrated Mr. Forbes might get in the time it would take to get there and back. Rosa glanced at Charlene, who sat in her designated chair. She was quite likely the reason Mr. Post had had a lapse of memory regarding his prop, though her expression remained demure and guilt-free. Apparently, Charlene *could be* a good actress.

Dennis from props appeared at a sprint. He stopped and held out the gun, too winded to talk.

Nicholas Post snatched the gun away, only offering a small nod to Dennis, who then stumbled out of the shot.

Mr. Forbes called, "Roll the camera! Let's do this once. Let's do it right!"

Mr. Salvatore called for "Background Action", and all the extras in the vicinity mimed with their mouths and bodies, not making any sound. Rosa and Gloria did the same. As before, Bernie crossed toward them and mimed along with them right as Mr. Forbes called, "Action!"

This time, Charlene's line was loud and clear from behind the camera. Scott Huntington swung down from the balcony and banged against the saloon railing. Rosa let out an involuntary gasp and then held a hand to her chest as Mr. Huntington whooshed through the small town, zigzagging as he had been told. Stunties went flying, and Rosa wondered exactly how hard Mr. Huntington had pushed them, or were they simply trained to make their falls big and bold?

Everything moved quickly with Nicholas Post in the chase. He delivered his line, "Dirk! Stop, or I'll shoot."

Mr. Huntington turned and displayed his first smile of the day, cocky and smug. As if daring Mr. Post to take a shot, he held out his hands to the sides. When he turned, Mr. Post stopped on his X, held up the revolver in his hand, and aimed. The shot rang out so loudly that Gloria let out an involuntary scream. Bernie held a hand over his mouth and then turned his feigned horror toward Mr. Huntington's stumbling body.

Mr. Huntington stumbled forward, fell to his knees, his face expressing shock and pain. Not only that, but he popped his blood pack in the middle of his chest, rather than where he had been instructed to—his shoulder.

Letting out another groan, the actor fell to the ground, face-first. Mr. Huntington was quite a stuntman. Rosa now understood what everyone meant about his propensity to overact—especially when Mr. Post ran onto the scene, and Mr. Huntington still hadn't gotten up from his collapsed position so they could finish the chase.

Mr. Forbes called, "Cut!"

Enraged, Mr. Post said, "I can't work with this! Even delaying my entrance by twenty seconds isn't going to work if this guy is going to overplay everything!"

Mr. Forbes rushed onto the scene. "Calm down, Nick," he murmured, but now Rosa and Gloria were close enough they could hear every word. "Remember, the press is here."

As though that was a code word, Mr. Post stood up a little straighter, and a seemingly genuine smile appeared on his face. "We'll get it next time," he said to Mr. Forbes. It didn't seem as much like a promise as a warning.

Mr. Forbes patted Mr. Post on the shoulder. "Take a break. I'll handle this."

As soon as Mr. Post walked away, Mr. Forbes turned to Scott Huntington, still splayed out facedown on the road as though he knew exactly how badly he had blown it.

"Come on, let's rehearse this thing so we can get it right." Frederick Forbes was no longer trying to keep the exhaustion out of his voice.

Mr. Huntington still didn't move. Rosa noticed something near the side of his shirt at the waist. It looked like blood leaking out, and she had to wonder exactly how big those blood packs were.

Mr. Forbes tapped the stunt actor with his shoe, and when the man didn't move, Rosa felt her blood chill.

Scott Huntington had really been shot!

8

On Mr. Forbes' instructions, Mr. Salvatore picked up a bullhorn and yelled, "Everyone off the set! Everyone off the set!"

Mr. Forbes reached for Mr. Huntington's shoulder, but Rosa caught him by the arm and shook her head. "You shouldn't touch him," she said as she grabbed a fistful of her crinoline and knelt beside Mr. Huntington's prone form. She placed two fingers on the side of the man's neck.

Gloria ran to Rosa's side. "What's going on?"

"Mr. Huntington appears to have been shot with a real bullet."

Mr. Forbes' bushy brows furrowed in confusion. "Is he—?"

Rosa glanced up. "I can't find a pulse."

A few moments later, John Salvatore stormed over. "Off the set, ladies!" he demanded.

Addressing the director and his assistant, Rosa said, "I'm Rosa Reed, of Reed Investigations and a former constable of the London Metropolitan Police Force. I may be of some assistance until the police arrive."

"The police?" John Salvatore's eyebrows pulled together in annoyance.

"Yes. The man's been shot," Rosa said. "Does anyone know where the gun is?"

The seriousness of the situation seemed to settle on the assistant director. He looked in several directions before he finally answered, "Dennis should have it by now. But it was filled with blanks. We used the same gun for rehearsal."

"I recommend you keep everyone back, get security here as soon as possible, and make certain of where that gun is now. I suspect the police will want to question Mr. Post and your crew members in charge of props."

Looking to Mr. Forbes, who nodded slowly, Mr. Salvatore took off into the crowd. Members of the crew in the surrounding circle called out. "What happened?" and "Is he okay?"

"Please keep your distance for the moment," Rosa said. "We have to make sure the medic can get through as soon as he arrives."

One of the men that Rosa had noticed earlier from the press persisted, "Is Mr. Huntington okay?"

Ignoring the press, Rosa surveyed Scott Huntington's body from all sides, looking for any other evidence of what had occurred. The trail of blood was growing.

The film medic pushed through the crowd and ran over. "What happened?"

"I believe he was shot," Rosa said.

"Yes. They were using blanks." He checked for a pulse, first at the wrist and then the neck.

"That blood is real," Rosa said.

The medic took a sniff and looked at her. "So it is. Normally, it's just colored water."

Sirens sounded in the distance, growing closer, and the medic said, "Not much I can do except wait for the ambulance."

Rosa agreed. She wasn't sure what had happened, but it appeared to be a crime scene, and if this man was already dead, there was no need to move him until the police and the medical examiner arrived.

Soon the emergency vehicles drove onto set, and the crowds were forced back further. Detective Miguel Belmonte and his partner, Detective Bill Sanchez, who always looked like he'd just got out of bed, stepped out of their vehicle. They were followed by Officer Richardson, the police photographer, who had arrived in a separate patrol car.

It didn't matter the seriousness of the situation. Seeing Miguel always made Rosa's heart race: The way his suit fit his athletic form with a crisp white shirt and narrow black tie. How his fedora sat on the crown of his short black hair. His warm, dark eyes and milk-coffee colored skin, and when he smiled, those dang dimples!

She fortified herself, calling forth every molecule of professionalism.

His expression twisted indiscernibly as his gaze moved from her pouffed-up hair, across her corseted bodice, along her netted legs, down to her high-heeled shoes, then back to her face.

"Rosa?"

Rosa didn't blame him for not immediately recognizing her.

"I know. I'm like a bad rash." It was a poorly executed joke, but Rosa did seem thrust into Miguel's orbit more than could be called coincidentally. He frowned, but his eyes traveled along the length of Rosa's barely clothed body. Rosa's face grew warm, and she overlapped her arms across her chest.

"Gloria asked me to join her as an extra for today's shoot." It had been meant to be fun and a diversion from another boring day sitting around her office. Well, she was no longer bored. "This man died during production." She nodded at the figure on the dusty road.

The film medic joined them. "There's no pulse. I believe he was shot."

"The gun was supposed to have blanks," Rosa said.

"Where's the gun now?" Miguel asked.

Mr. Forbes stepped in. "I'm the director, Frederick Forbes. My assistant is fetchin' the prop and should be back shortly. And you are?"

"Detective Belmonte and—" Miguel nodded at his partner who hovered over the body, his wrinkled tie hanging loose from its clip. "—that's Detective Sanchez and Officer Richardson."

Officer Richardson scowled when he saw Rosa. Though she'd proven herself useful to the police in the past, Officer Richardson had never warmed to her. He didn't approve of women doing a man's job, something he'd implied to Rosa on more than one occasion.

Rosa didn't want him to get a good look at her assets so turned her back to him, though her ruffled behind didn't help. She pinched her lips when she heard him chuckle at her expense.

Miguel, focusing on the director, said, "Can you walk me through what happened?"

Mr. Forbes described the last take. "I thought he'd gone off script; he liked to improvise."

Miguel removed a notepad from his suit pocket and jotted notes.

Rosa startled at the sound of Larry's voice. "I hear we have a body!"

"Howdy, Detectives," he said to Miguel and Detective Sanchez.

"Rayburn," Miguel said with a tip of his hat.

Larry's gaze settled on Rosa, his eyes taking in her risqué costume as his voice pitched upward in question. "Rosa, such an unexpected turn of events, huh?"

"Yes," Rosa said. "Gloria and I were on the set when it happened." She glanced around for Gloria. Where *was* her cousin, anyway?

Mr. Forbes introduced himself again. "I'm the director of this film."

"Dr. Rayburn," Larry returned, extending a hand in greeting. "Assistant medical examiner." He then turned to the body and began his examination.

Rosa joined him after a moment. "What do you think?"

"Quite clearly, a gunshot wound. Probably the cause of death. Did you see him fall?"

"Yes," Rosa said. "He dropped to his knees then slowly keeled over. It looked like a bad performance."

"It's possible he had a heart attack or an underlying medical condition," Larry said, "but the wound is directly over his heart. No surviving that."

Despite Rosa's efforts to ignore Miguel, it seemed she had an internal radar that she just couldn't shut off. Over Larry's shoulder, she caught sight of Charlene rushing toward Miguel and flinging herself into his arms, "I am so glad you're here! This is awful."

Although Charlene had a handkerchief out and was dabbing her eyes, Rosa could see no tears.

Great performance! Rosa thought, then chastised herself inwardly immediately for being petty.

"Rosa?"

Had Larry said something? "I'm sorry, what?"

"I know this is a strange moment, but . . . dinner later?"

Rosa's eyes flickered to Miguel, who held one of Charlene's traitorous hands while consoling her.

"Yes, Larry," Rosa said. "I'd love that."

More police officers in blue double-breasted uniforms arrived on set, and Rosa overheard Miguel instruct some officers to search the area for a bullet and others to locate the prop pistol. Miguel had left Charlene, the *cheater,* with the director. She looked oh-so-demure in her high-collared blouse and upswept hair. Miguel cast a glance over his shoulder as she walked off the set, presumably to return to her trailer and remove her costume.

Rosa, once again aware of her exposed cleavage, was quite eager to do the same—turn and walk away.

Despite the inclination to roll into herself to minimize her bosom, she stood straight with shoulders back, the posture she'd had trained into her at the Metropolitan Police Training School.

Miguel showed professional restraint, keeping his gaze locked on her eyes. "You're free to go, Rosa."

Rosa felt the weight of her fake eyelashes as she blinked in response. He was dismissing her. *Of course, he was.* She wasn't an officer of the law in Santa Bonita, and even though she and Miguel had worked together on other cases, it didn't mean she should automatically assume she'd be invited to consult on this case. However, she *had been* on the scene and a witness.

Miguel glanced over his shoulder to the spot Charlene had just vacated, and Rosa understood. *Charlene doesn't want Miguel to work with me.*

Rosa didn't blame her. She and Charlene hadn't exactly gotten off on the right foot, even if Miguel hadn't shared the story of their romantic history with her. Being female, Charlene could undoubtedly sense the attraction. No, the *former* attraction.

"Of course," Rosa said. Challenging why Miguel had dismissed her would only cause a scene, and Rosa wasn't about to risk her reputation by behaving in an unseemly fashion.

Larry packed up his doctor's bag. "I'm finished

here, Detective," he said. "I'll schedule an autopsy as soon as possible."

"Thank you, Doctor," Miguel returned. He tipped his hat to Rosa before pivoting away.

"I'll walk you, Rosa," Larry said. His eyes scanned her outfit once again, and his lips pulled up into an amused grin. "I assume you have a place to change?"

"The wardrobe tent has curtained-off areas."

Rosa was relieved to find Gloria there, already changed out of her costume. "Oh, Rosa, finally! I'm exhausted, and my feet ache from these shoes. I told the wardrobe assistant that they were too small. Oh, Dr. Rayburn, hi."

"Hello, Miss Forrester, how are ya?"

"I'm fine, thank you, except for the dramatic circumstances."

"Shockin', I'm sure." Larry gave Rosa a quick kiss on the cheek. "I'll pick you up at seven."

"See you then," Rosa said. Both she and Gloria watched Larry stroll away.

Gloria sighed. "You're so lucky, Rosa. Such a gentleman!"

Rosa had to agree. She just had to get her heart to line up with her head.

9

Rosa loved the private bathroom attached to her bedroom at the Forrester mansion. Painted a lovely green, with a white freestanding porcelain tub and black-and-white tile floor, Rosa found the room a soothing place to think. Soaking in the steamy water of her bath gave her mind a chance to roam, and soon her thoughts replayed the events of the shooting.

The first person I'll interview will be the props man, Dennis McCann. He had the means and opportunity to swap the blanks with a real bullet, but why? Motive was important. Miguel could run that down without my help.

On set, tension between Nicholas Post and Scott Huntington had been obvious. Their ongoing feud over their mutual dislike of one another had been fodder for the tabloids for some time. Rosa had thought that perhaps it was a marketing gimmick to keep both names in the minds of moviegoers and drive them to see *Quick Strike* when it released.

But perhaps a proud man like Mr. Post didn't relish sharing the spotlight. He seemed the type who had to possess the best roles, the top publicity, and apparently, the leading lady.

Rosa blew at the bath bubbles, which slowly dissipated. *What on earth am I supposed to do with what I saw? Tell Miguel? Anyone in their right mind knows getting involved in another couple's romantic life is akin to stepping on a powder keg.*

But could she watch him marry someone she knew wasn't faithful? Miguel was her friend, if nothing more, and what kind of friend would keep that information to herself? But telling him was sure to destroy any semblance of friendship they had, as delicate as it seemed. Plus, they lived and worked in the same town, and their paths would inevitably cross. Rosa didn't want to make an enemy out of Miguel Belmonte.

She let out a defeated breath as she reached for the drain plug with her toes. Thoughts of Miguel had dominated her mind enough. She had to get ready to spend the rest of the evening with Larry Rayburn. *He* was the one she should be thinking about.

Her toes found the chain, tugged the rubber plug

out of position, and the swirling sound of the now tepid water draining filled the room. Wrapping a large towel around her body and a smaller one over her hair, Rosa stepped into her bedroom and to the built-in closet across from a king-size canopy bed. Diego stretched out languidly in the center. He licked his forepaw with determination, apparently bathing as well.

Rosa scrubbed his soft furry head before settling into the chair that faced her antique vanity dresser. Sitting carefully on the edge of her chair, she brushed her short hair, drew curlers out of her drawer one at a time, rolled up small sections, and attached them in place with a plastic pin. The process required a certain finesse as rolling too tightly caused hair-pulling pain and too loosely risked them falling out or failing to produce a suitable curl.

When she finished securing the last one, she picked up a mirror—its back matching the swan design of her brush—and examined the back of her head.

"Looks good, Diego."

Rosa chuckled at Diego's look of disinterest. She'd gotten into the habit of talking to her kitten, which was fine, so long as he didn't talk back!

As Rosa turned to close her curler drawer, her eye landed on an envelope that didn't belong in there. Picking it up with two fingers, she frowned at the address. Written in the neat cursive style of her former fiancé, Lord Winston Eveleigh, the letter evoked the memories of frustration on the day this third letter had arrived. He had begged—*no demanded*—her to return to London. And he'd included veiled threats of ruining her reputation or such rot. She'd slammed it into the wrong drawer. Standing, she walked over to her desk, opened the top drawer, and placed the letter on the others.

Rosa turned to Diego, who looked at her curiously. "I'm not sure why I'm keeping these."

The statement wasn't exactly true. Something niggled at the back of her brain, a caution she might need them as insurance or proof of harassment one day, though she dearly hoped not.

Rosa plugged in her portable hairdryer, set the base on her dresser, and stretched out the pink accordion hose attached to the dome headpiece. She carefully situated the dome over her head then turned the machine on.

She found both the hum of the dryer and its warm air soothing and closed her eyes. Encountering Winston's letters caused her mind to return to London. She missed her parents, Basil and Ginger Reed, and Hartigan House, her childhood home, but she didn't miss Britain. Perhaps it was because Winston waited there to torment her, or, rather more likely, it was the deeper pain of his sister Vivien Eveleigh's unsolved murder.

Rosa and Lady Vivien—Vivien hated it when Rosa called her *"Lady"*—had gone to school together and were the best of friends. During the war, they were separated for a time, when Rosa had been sent to live with Aunt Louisa, and Vivien and Winston had gone to Canada, but when they reunited afterward, it was like no time between them had passed.

Her death had shaken Rosa to the core. That her murder had remained unsolved had been a strong impetus for Rosa to join the London Metropolitan Police. With her parents involved in detective work, she hadn't experienced social pressure to pursue something typically more feminine, as other young girls would have.

Vivien's death was the event that had catapulted her into Winston's arms. There were five years between the Eveleigh siblings, so Rosa hadn't seen a lot of Vivien's older brother when they were growing up.

An emotional crisis had pulled them together, but deep down, Rosa knew it was a bad decision, which was why she had kept putting off setting the date.

Winston had finally lost patience and booked a wedding date without her knowledge. Once the invitations had been sent out, Rosa's anxiety over her decision heightened, but as each day the wedding grew closer, Rosa felt like she had no choice but to go through with it. And once her relatives from California had arrived in London, Rosa was resigned to her fate.

It was her father, Basil Reed, who had given her a way out. They had been in the narthex of the church waiting for the march to begin.

"It's not too late," he said.

"What?"

"It's only too late once you say the words 'I do'."

Rosa couldn't believe her ears. Her mother had never been a big fan of Winston but had always said it was Rosa's life and her decision. And Rosa had made her decision. She just didn't think she could change her mind.

Winston had watched her as Rosa stepped slowly toward the altar, his eyes not filled with love, but conquest. When she'd got to the front, she'd turned to her father, "Dad?"

He knew. He knew.

Basil Reed had taken her arm and turned her, so she faced the back door.

Rosa had hitched up her hem and run.

The timer on the dryer pinged, snapping Rosa out of her reverie. So far, she had spent her time preparing for her dinner with Larry thinking about two men who weren't Larry!

Rosa lifted the dryer dome off her hair, now dry,

plucked out the pins, and unrolled the curlers. She brushed out the curls, patted them into place, and added a heavy mist of hair spray.

"That should do it." Next, she attended to her makeup. First up, a puff of powder, a shade darker than her natural pale tone. She patted every inch of her face with a large duster. After that, a light-pink rouge to highlight the cheekbones. A shadow for the lids followed a brown eyeliner. Rosa chose a soft green to match her dress.

Picking up her eyebrow pencil, also a shade darker than her normal brow color, she penciled in her brows, creating a nice arch. Applying the cake mascara was Rosa's least favorite makeup application. It had taken years to master the mini, flat brush, and to keep from getting crumbs of mascara in her eye, but the result—bigger, brighter-looking eyes—made the effort worth it.

Finally, lipstick. Rosa gravitated to pinks and orange, saving red for special occasions.

Rosa stood in front of her closet, enjoying the built-in feature of the room. *Why do Europeans still insist on separate furniture pieces to do the job?* She glanced at Diego, who watched her now as if he was about to pounce. "What shall I wear, little boy?" Pointing at her eye makeup, she added, "I've already decided on something green."

Flipping through the options, she chose a jade-green pencil dress with a square neckline and wide pockets on the hips.

Rosa added a pearl choker and had clipped on the second matching earring when she heard the doorbell chime. She checked her wristwatch.

"He's early, Diego."

Her cat turned onto his back with his front legs stretched out front, the very picture of lazy feline indifference.

"Thanks for caring." Rosa ruffled Diego's ears, but he didn't move a muscle except for his tail, which wagged in annoyed response.

Hurriedly, she slipped on black pumps and grabbed the purse she'd used earlier—too late to move her items over to another one now—and headed down the curving staircase.

But it wasn't Larry waiting with Bledsoe, the butler, at the entrance, but Clarence's estranged wife, Vanessa. Beside her, looking sad and vulnerable, was their little four-year-old daughter, Julie.

"Is Clarence here," Vanessa said rather robotically as she patted her short honey-blonde hair, which was backcombed on top, and the tips flipped up. "I phoned earlier, but he wouldn't take my call."

Rosa thought it highly unlikely that Clarence would purposely refuse to accept a call from Vanessa, especially since little Julie lived with her most of the time.

Rosa approached, keeping her tone light. "Hi, Vanessa. Hi, Julie! What a surprise."

"Where's Clarence?"

Vanessa had never shown Rosa much warmth, but she seemed cooler than usual.

Bledsoe replied, "He's gone out for the evening, Mrs. Forrester. Would you like to leave a message?"

"Or come in!" Rosa said. Vanessa and Aunt Louisa were hardly on speaking terms, but it didn't erase the fact that Vanessa was family.

Panic flashed behind Vanessa's eyes, causing Rosa to feel alert. "Is everything all right?" Rosa said. "Would you like to come in for a cup of tea or a bit of brandy?"

Vanessa swallowed. "I need Clarence to take Julie for a little while. Just a while."

Rosa felt real concern for her former cousin's emotional state. "Of course, Julie can stay here." It wasn't Rosa's place as extended family to offer, but she couldn't imagine Aunt Louisa turning her granddaughter away.

"I'll fetch Mrs. Forrester," Bledsoe said.

Vanessa knelt and embraced Julie with an alarming ferociousness. When she pulled away, a tear traced along her cheek. "Be good," was all she said before racing out the door.

Rosa ran after her, "Vanessa!" The wheels of Vanessa's black Pontiac sedan spit up dirt as she flew down the drive.

Rosa slowly closed the door and turned to the frightened little girl who stood alone in the foyer, her lip pushed out in a pout.

"Julie," Rosa said gently and took the little girl's soft hand in hers. "Everything is fine. We're so pleased you've come to stay. Won't Daddy be surprised?"

Julie bravely swallowed back a sob.

Aunt Louisa appeared at that moment. "Oh, Julie. Come to Grandma." Julie ran into Aunt Louisa's arms, and for a moment, Rosa witnessed a soft side to her aunt's normally brisk persona.

The doorbell rang again, and this time it was Larry. Rosa offered him a smile as they hugged each other. She silently hoped that Clarence would return home soon.

10

The next morning in her office, Rosa busied herself, putting on a pot of coffee and cleaning cups and saucers. Her mind flipped back and forth between the lovely time she had had with Larry the evening before and the look of consternation on Clarence's face when he'd learned about Vanessa dropping Julie off unceremoniously at the Forrester mansion. Fortunately, Gloria had been home and was always more than up to entertaining her little niece.

Rosa, at the window, stared blankly at the busy street below as she waited for the coffee to brew. Her mind and emotions seemed scattered after yesterday's events, and she was glad that her morning wasn't yet planned out. Perhaps she would just spend part of it sitting in her office reading her novel or listening to music. She regarded her office. It still felt incomplete to her, but she couldn't decide what was missing. Perhaps a plant or two to add to the ambiance? But with her track record, dying plants did little to make a room feel cozy.

A record player with its suitcase-style lid opened was nicely displayed on a sideboard, and Rosa flicked through her selection of LPs. She chose an album she'd just picked up a few days ago, called *The Ames Brothers*, removed the vinyl from the cardboard sleeve, placed it on the record player, and set the needle on the record's edge.

The first song, "Not You, Not I", had a wonderful, lilting rhythm that made Rosa smile. She sashayed across the floor with an invisible partner who formed slowly in her imagination into Miguel. They'd often danced together back in the forties, and The Ames Brothers' style recalled the music that was popular then. Perhaps that was why she liked this record so much.

Thinking of Miguel brought the death of Scott Huntington to mind. She wondered how Miguel and Detective Sanchez were getting along. None of her business. Besides, she had other things to think about.

The song ended, as did her dance. She poured herself a mug of freshly brewed coffee then leaned back in her office chair.

"No more thoughts about, uh, that man, or that

case," she said for Diego's benefit. Her cat opened one eye as he slept on a chair in front of her desk. "Let me tell you about the date I had with Larry last night." She took a sip of coffee, then continued. "He took me to a quaint Italian restaurant, and we ate cheesy lasagna and drank a bottle of Chianti. For dessert, we had strawberry ice cream." She grouped her fingertips, brought them to pursed lips, and smacked them. "Delectable. And Larry's such a nice man, Diego. He really is."

Who was she trying to convince? Of course, Larry was a nice man. That wasn't to be debated. Her problem lay with the "bomb" he'd dropped on her over their final drink.

The dinner had been lovely—candlelight on red-and-white-checkered tablecloths, classical music playing from a stereo in the corner. The scent of strong cheese and garlic, fresh tomatoes and lemons, and herbs like basil and oregano tantalized their senses. Larry looked as charming as ever, regaling her with tales from the south. What a wild and exotic place! Alligators roamed free!

"You should see your face, darlin'," Larry had said with a glint in his eye.

"I think I would be terrified to live there."

"It's not like reptiles and snakes rule the land though. Especially in cities like Galveston, you'd be hard-pressed to find a scaled-backed creature roaming the streets."

"When it comes to wild creatures, Britain is rather benign," Rosa had said. "We have foxes and deer, but nothing too terrifying."

"California may not have roaming alligators," Larry said, "but you'd be surprised at how many bears live in the hills, and I've heard they can be quite dangerous."

"I suppose," Rosa consented. She'd never seen a real bear.

Larry had stared back apologetically. "I didn't mean to scare ya. Galveston has got a lot to offer. Like here, it has wonderful beaches and piers."

He'd reached over the checkered tablecloth and taken Rosa's hand. "You mean the world to me, Rosa, and well, I have something to say."

Rosa's heart had jumped into her throat. *He wasn't about to propose, was he?*

She'd let out a breath when his next words went in a different direction. "I've been offered the job of Chief Medical Examiner in Galveston."

Rosa had inhaled sharply. The implications of Larry's announcement had landed like an anvil on glass. "You're leaving?"

"Not yet. Not until November." Color had filled his cheeks as he continued. "I'm hoping you'll think about moving there too. I feel like we are just beginning, but I think we have somethin' special. If you move to Galveston, we can see where it takes us. I can help you set up a new office there."

Not a proposal, but almost. Wait. Was it a proposal? Oh dear.

"Oh," was all she'd managed in response.

"No need to decide today." Larry had released Rosa's hand and busied himself with the bottle of wine, refilling their glasses. "There are two months ahead of us."

Rosa had been gobsmacked. She liked Larry, quite a lot, but she wasn't in love with him, not yet. She'd only just set up her office in Santa Bonita, and she had family here.

However, it wasn't like her business was booming, and she couldn't live with her aunt forever, could she?

Larry had raised his glass and stared intently into Rosa's eyes. "Just say you'll think about it."

Rosa had clinked her glass with his. "I will, Larry. I need some time, but I'll think about it."

Sighing, Rosa brought her thoughts back to the present. Deciding a good book was in order, she selected *The Body Snatchers*, perfect escapism reading, then got comfortable on the office couch. Stretching out her legs, putting her feet up on the coffee table, she opened the book, an instant signal to Diego that he should climb onto her lap and take up residence on the pages.

"Oh, you little rascal." Rosa scrubbed him under the chin. "You need all the attention, don't you?"

Rosa hardly expected her pet to answer, and neither did she expect the knock at the door. Rosa flung her feet back to the floor, pushed Diego and the book onto the couch, and called out, "Come in!"

The door swung open, and Rosa would have been lying if she hadn't admitted to being surprised by the person standing there.

"Miss Williamson," Rosa said, hoping the shock she felt hadn't registered on her face.

Rosa claimed her desk chair while motioning for Nicholas Post's secretary to take one of the empty chairs facing it. Miss Williamson was a thin waif of a thing, with red hair that reminded Rosa of her mother's hair.

The secretary glanced around the room. "This is a nice office, Miss Reed. You must be doing all right here in Santa Bonita".

"Thank you," Rosa said. "I'm just getting started. It takes time."

Miss Williamson took the chair and sat upright, clasping her purse with her gloved hands as it rested on her lap. "I understand you were a police officer in London?"

"That's correct. I came to Santa Bonita to visit my relatives, but then decided to stay." Rosa gestured toward the kitchenette. "I have fresh coffee in the pot. Can I offer you some?"

"No, that's fine. I would rather just get down to business if you don't mind."

"Certainly." Rosa was more than eager to learn what Nicholas Post's secretary had to say.

"As you've probably surmised," Miss Williamson said carefully, "I'm here on Mr. Post's behalf."

Rosa lowered her chin and waited for Miss Williamson to continue.

"The police are treating Mr. Post like a prime suspect. It's just awful, Miss Reed. Mr. Post wouldn't hurt a flea."

Rosa wasn't so sure about that but stayed silent.

Miss Williamson clasped the fingers of her gloved hands together. "Mr. Post needs someone to help him get ahead of this. Help to prove that he had nothing to do with this incident, show he is innocent beyond a shadow of a doubt. I fear it's too late to stop the tabloids, but we have to try to clear his name before any real damage is done."

"I see. And how does that involve me?"

The secretary leaned in. "I want to hire you on Mr. Post's behalf. I know you're fairly new to Santa Bonita, but you've already got a reputation for solving difficult cases, even though you're a woman."

Rosa ignored the slight. It was commonly accepted, even by other women, that females in the 1950s worked primarily as teachers, secretaries, or nurses until marriage, then stayed at home to raise the children.

"Let me ask you a question, Miss Williamson." Rosa leaned forward on her desk. "If you were to pick someone on the set who would have a motive to kill Scott Huntington, who would that be?"

Miss Williamson seemed like she was prepared for the question and answered straight away. "I can't say so with one hundred percent certainty, but I suspect Pam Vickers. She is one of the main hairdressers."

"Oh?"

"Pam is a well-known hairstylist. She has done hair for many famous people. In fact, she and Scott Huntington were, you know . . ." She put her gloved hands into the air to form quotation marks. ". . . having a fling." Although I don't know how anyone could be in a relationship with a man like that."

"How long ago was that?"

"It ended about three weeks ago, I think, and not exactly on a good note. There was a scene in the hairdressing trailer. He yelled out some nasty things about her in front of a bunch of crew members and extras.

She ran out crying. Anyways, later I overheard her talking to some of the other hairdressers about it."

Rosa just looked at Miss Williamson and waited.

"She said something about how Scott Huntington had better be thankful that she didn't blab about her love life, especially to her family."

"What does that mean?"

Miss Williamson just shrugged, "I am not sure; I don't know the woman that well. But it certainly is suspicious, don't you think?"

Rosa would concede that it was an interesting line of inquiry.

"Miss Reed, are you willing to take the case?"

Rosa hesitated. Working for a suspect would quite likely cross professional lines that Miguel would find upsetting.

Miss Williamson misinterpreted the pause. "We can pay your fee. That's not an issue."

"No, it's not . . ."

Impatiently, Miss Williamson pressed, "Then what? Mr. Post is anxious to get started. His reputation is on the line. Please say you will."

Rosa could understand Mr. Post's plight. She'd read articles in magazines about celebrity antics, like a pair who played the best of friends on screen but loathed each other behind closed doors, or some who had not-so-secret affairs—*oh dear, what if Mr. Post's dalliance with Charlene Winters got out? The humiliation for Miguel would be devastating. Rosa would do anything to prevent that from happening.*

She locked her gaze on Miss Williamson. "I'll do it."

11

Rosa parked her Corvette next to the police vehicles sitting at the gate of the movie set. The entrance was partitioned off by rope. Officer Richardson, the man who Rosa was now sure must be Santa Bonita's surliest officer, stood guard.

"Hello, Officer Richardson."

"Hello, Miss Reed."

"Is Detective Belmonte on set?"

"Not yet, ma'am, but we are expecting him any minute. The area's closed to the public until further notice. Only employees of the production company are allowed."

Peering beyond the officer's shoulders, Rosa could see the eerily empty street—a sharp contrast to the busyness of the day before. A lot of the talent and crew were staying at the Santa Bonita Starburst Hotel, but, according to Mary Williamson, the police had asked if everyone would come back to the set during working hours for at least an extra day to accommodate the investigation.

"I'm here to see Mr. Post in an official capacity," Rosa said. "Please let him know I'm waiting."

"Yes, ma'am." The officer spoke to another officer nearby, and the second one left, presumably to run Rosa's errand. She wanted to speak to Mr. Post, but first, out of courtesy, she should let Miguel know that she'd been hired by the actor. Staying in Miguel's goodwill would only make her job easier.

"I'd also like to speak to Detective Belmonte when he gets here," Rosa began. "I have information he'd want to know."

"Yes, ma'am," The officer said again, but just then, Miguel arrived in an unmarked police car. He stepped out with purpose but slowed when his dark eyes met Rosa's. There was a brief flash of irritation on his face before he relaxed into a smile.

"Miss Reed," he said politely. "Why am I not surprised to see you here?"

The officer responded for her. "Miss Reed says she has information about the case, Detective."

"Of course she does." He nodded for Rosa to follow him out of earshot of the officers guarding the entrance.

"I suspect you couldn't keep your nose out of a police case even if someone paid you to stay away."

"Call it serendipity if you must," Rosa replied, feeling miffed. Miguel was behaving in a prickly manner, and she wouldn't be surprised if his fiancée and her cheating lips were behind it.

Miguel ducked his chin. "What gives?"

"I've been hired by Mary Williamson on behalf of Nicholas Post to clear his name. I thought you should know."

Miguel frowned. "He's a suspect. A prime suspect, I might add."

"Which is why I thought you should know."

"Are you always going to be a thorn in my flesh, Rosa?"

Rosa smirked. "I don't think I can help it."

Miguel let out a frustrated breath. "As they say, if you can't beat 'em, join 'em."

"Exactly," Rosa replied. "We're after the same end. I've been hired to prove my client's innocence if he is indeed innocent, and you want to find the real killer. We might as well work together."

Miguel shrugged with a look of concession. "I'm headed to the props trailer to talk to Mr. McCann."

Relieved at Miguel's change of heart, Rosa said, "I'll join you."

Mr. Post approached just at that moment, casting a

disparaging stare Miguel's way before smiling at Rosa. "Miss Reed. Good to see you! Miss Williamson phoned to share the fantastic news. You will prove my innocence, I can feel it, to the police and my fans."

Rosa stretched out her gloved hand. "Mr. Post, I just wanted to confirm with you that you had, indeed, commissioned Miss Williamson to seek me out."

"*Indeed*," Mr. Post said with a chuckle. "Your accent is adorable, Miss Reed."

Rosa's face muscles tightened. She wanted Miguel to see that her client was serious about their arrangement, and blatant flirtation wasn't how to do it.

"Yes, well," Rosa started stiffly, "now that you've given your verbal assurance, I'll call at your trailer to confirm the contract." The papers were in her purse ready for Mr. Post to sign. "If you'd be so kind as to excuse me for the moment?"

Mr. Post's eyes darted between Rosa and Miguel, and a large grin crossed his face. "Of course. Do your job, Miss Reed. We'll talk soon."

The actor strolled away with an abundance of confidence, and Rosa hoped that some of that was placed in her ability to do what she had been hired to do.

She just hoped that Mr. Post wasn't Scott Huntington's killer.

. . .

Any concern Rosa had that Mr. Forbes might recognize her from her extra work the day before evaporated the moment she stepped into the film's director trailer. His bulbous eyes registered confusion as to why this strange woman was with the detective in charge. Rosa was out of costume and figured her outfit—a pink swing dress patterned with large white polka dots—had thrown him off.

"Detective," Mr. Forbes said, looking at Miguel. "Have you found our man?"

"Not so quick as that," Miguel said. "We're doing all that we can, but I'm here to question the witnesses."

"Again? Didn't you folks do that yesterday? I understand you've asked us all to remain here on set."

"Yes, and I am thankful for your compliance. There are a lot of people to interview. And in my experience, the mind needs time to process a tragedy, especially one witnessed firsthand. It's not uncommon for people to later remember details that they'd forgotten on the day."

"Sure, sure." He nodded at Rosa. "Who's this?"

Rosa stepped forward with one extended hand. "I'm Miss Rosa Reed, of Reed Investigations. I consult with the Santa Bonita Police on occasion."

There was no need to reveal that the director's leading man had hired her. "I also must disclose that I was on set yesterday as an extra."

Mr. Forbes squinted as his mind worked then his eyes rounded with recognition. "You were one of the saloon girls!"

"That's right."

Miguel removed a notepad from his suit jacket pocket. "Have you worked with these same heads of crew before, Mr. Forbes?" Miguel flipped pages as he referred to his notes. "Mr. McCann, the props master; Mr. Salvatore, the assistant director; and Miss Vickers in hairdressing?"

"All but Mr. Salvatore," Mr. Forbes said, his thick mustache twitching like a small mammal perched on his upper lip. "My regular AD had a car accident just before we went to production. Broke both legs. John Salvatore was brought in by the studio last minute. I didn't have any choice in the matter."

Rosa had her own set of notes, which she removed from her bag. Once Miss Williamson had left her office that morning, she'd taken the time to jot down what she remembered from the crime scene—before and after Mr. Huntington had been gunned down.

"You visited Mr. Post's trailer during the break, correct?"

"I already told the police this yesterday, but yes, I did. I dropped off some script notes for him. Not that he read them, I would wager."

"Did you notice the revolver?"

"Yes, I did. It was there."

"But you didn't touch it."

"I did not, and more to the point, I did not replace those blanks with real bullets. I'm not a gun guy. Never owned one." He turned to Miguel. "Did they find the bullet, Detective?"

Rosa was interested in the answer to that question.

Miguel gave a quick shake of his head. "Not yet. It's possible the perpetrator managed to pick it up."

Rosa concurred. "Once everyone realized what had happened, the set turned rather chaotic."

"Have you and Mr. Post worked together before?" Miguel asked.

Rosa already knew that the two headstrong men had done a couple of films together, and she assumed Miguel was probing for a possible motive.

"Yes, several times. The last time was on the set of *The Last Clue*, which I understand was showing here in Santa Bonita just recently."

Rosa decided not to mention she had seen the film, partly because she didn't want to be asked what she thought of the acting. "Look, I can admit that Scott was a pain in the a . . ." His focus zoomed to Rosa, "A pain in the behind to work with. As if I didn't have an artistic bone in my body, he questioned all of my decisions, but—"

"Yes?" Miguel prompted.

"Well, if you're looking at me as a possible suspect, I can tell you that I wouldn't have killed him even just for the simple reason that stopping the shoot would cost too much money—*is costing* too much money. If you'd like to have a look at our financials, you'll soon see that this shutdown, if it lasts any amount of time, could put the entire studio's future in jeopardy.

"Besides, if I killed every actor that I didn't like, I would be a mass murderer." He chuckled dryly and looked at Miguel. "I am hoping that we don't have to hold the cast and crew here on set for any length of time—that alone costs thousands per day."

If Mr. Forbes' account was true, and the money trail would be among the first things the police would check out, then it left the director with a weak motive.

Unless there was more to the story.

"I don't anticipate having to keep everyone here very long," Miguel offered.

"Can you tell us about your history with Dennis McCann?" Rosa asked.

Mr. Forbes shrugged. "I've worked with him a dozen times or so. Every time a film has firearms, he's always my first choice for that, but I've even had him in for some of the more complicated props too. He's the kind of guy ya can count on, and if you think this whole thing is an accident, that somehow a real bullet was *mistakenly* used, I would vouch for Dennis

McCann one hundred times over. Besides, why would we even keep real bullets on a movie set? I wouldn't allow that.".

"Of course, you realize then," Miguel started, "that that would make this a definite murder case—"

"Not an accidental death." Rosa completed his sentence.

Mr. Forbes petted his mustache. "Yes, I realize that."

"Mr. McCann and Mr. Huntington seemed at odds on set yesterday?" Rosa asked.

"I certainly hope you're not basing your investigation on gruff personalities; if that were the case, we'd all be going to jail." He paused for a moment as if very reluctant to go on. "Dennis and Scott didn't have a lot of love for each other, that's true. Still, Dennis has worked with plenty of difficult actors, and they're all still alive." Mr. Forbes let out a dry laugh.

"Have Mr. McCann and Mr. Huntington ever had a physical altercation?" Miguel asked.

Mr. Forbes sat heavily in his desk chair. "I suppose you'll find out about this sooner or later. It was reported last year in *The Los Angeles Clandestine*. Those newspapers are the chicken scratchin's of bogus journalists trying to bait their readers with fantastical headlines."

Rosa wouldn't disagree with that statement.

"But," the director continued, "in this case, they got it right."

He leaned forward with his elbows on the desk, and his hands clasped together. Rosa had the distinct feeling that what he was about to say was something he had already planned to reveal, but was waiting for a detective to ask him about. He was a successful director. He knew how certain words should be timed and delivered for the utmost believability. Rosa poised her pen over her notebook.

Miguel hit his cue. "Can you elaborate?"

With a sigh of resignation, Mr. Forbes began. "On the set of *The Last Clue*, Scott Huntington and Dennis McCann came to blows. It took three crew members to pull them apart. Scott yelled at Dennis somethin' about the horse tack being substandard, and Dennis got madder than a hornet, takin' a strip off Scott in front of everyone.

"Scott walked right over to Dennis and gave him a knuckle sandwich on the jaw, sendin' him sprawling to the ground. Dennis pulled himself together, and I thought that was the end of it, but then he jumped Scott from behind. I wish I'd had the cameras rollin', 'cause it turned into a barn burner of a fight. Dennis got the worst of it. Scott's practiced in the art of fist-fightin'."

"How did it end?" Rosa asked.

"Like I said, it took three crew members to tear them apart. Dennis had a broken nose and a cracked rib and was in the hospital for two days. He had to finish the production with a nose brace and his chest wrapped. It was extremely humiliatin' for him. Especially after the story broke in *The Clandestine*."

It appeared to Rosa that more drama occurred off camera than on camera during film production.

12

The props master's trailer was significantly smaller than the one occupied by the director. Rosa moved as close to the wall as she could to make the diminutive space feel roomier. Miguel did the same.

"I need to ask a few questions, Mr. McCann," Miguel said. "Did anyone else have access to the gun that was used on set yesterday?"

"No. Like I said yesterday, production has to hire someone with specific weapons training when they have any kind of a gun on set, and that's me. Other props crew members have been specifically instructed to take care of the other props, but not the gun." Mr. McCann stood with his hands on his narrow hips, looking more angry than confused.

"It's normal in an investigation to be asked the

same question more than once, Mr. McCann," Miguel said as if sensing his irritation. "Now tell me about the gun; from the time you acquired it for this show until the last moment you saw it."

As if he was extremely inconvenienced, Mr. McCann raised an eyebrow nearly all the way to his hairline. "Fine," he said, plopping down into an empty chair. "At the first production meeting about *Quick Strike*, Forbes told me what kind of gun he wanted, especially for this particular scene."

Rosa thought it interesting that the director would be so specific, especially since he'd gone out of his way to tell them he knew nothing about guns. "Did you find it odd that Mr. Forbes was so specific?"

"Nah. This is a period piece. The guns have to suit the era. So, I brought in a few of my guns as samples and explained what each would be used for. They chose one and asked if they could pay me a gun rental fee rather than buying one for the film." Mr. McCann shrugged. "It's normal practice. They're always trying to save a buck."

"To confirm," Miguel said, "the gun used on the set yesterday was from your personal collection?"

Mr. McCann nodded. "I brought it in for our scheduled weapons training at the studio. I'm supposed to meet with the actors and actresses who interact with any of the guns on set, but Post snatched the thing out of my hand and said he knew how to use it. He flipped open the cylinder then turned away like he didn't have another minute to spare for me." Mr. McCann snorted. "I'm used to arrogant actors. I told him that if he didn't listen to my safety spiel, I'd be forced to tell the director he couldn't handle the gun. He glared at me, but he let me go over each of the steps of how it was loaded with gunpowder-only blank cartridges and how he could only aim at distances over twenty feet away."

"Why is that?" Miguel asked.

"The debris from a blank cartridge could still hurt someone or even be fatal."

"And he listened to all of this?" Miguel asked.

Mr. McCann let out a loud, single laugh. "I wouldn't call it listening, but he stood there smirking until I was done. Then he had a chance to fire off six rounds of blanks in an empty studio. Post knows his weapons and fired it like a pro. When I brought the gun for rehearsal yesterday, I was supposed to go over my safety speech once more, but he blew me off. Too proud to get direction from me when the extras and the crew were around."

The props master only confirmed what Rosa already knew about her client: Mr. Post was a proud, arrogant man.

"Is it usual for actors to use prop guns for rehearsal?" she asked.

"Not really, but Post is really finicky that way." Scoffing he added, "Says a dummy affects his acting style."

"What about Mr. Huntington?" Rosa asked. "Was he more agreeable?"

Mr. McCann blew a loud raspberry through his lips. "Scott was no better. My job was to tell him about the strength of the sound and how it would feel if he were truly shot. Not only was this supposed to help his acting . . ." He snorted again, ". . . but it was supposed to cue the shot for the camera so it would look realistic when he fell."

"And so, you handed over the gun to Mr. Post at rehearsal without much of a safety speech," Miguel confirmed.

"Not for lack of trying."

Miguel glanced at his notes. "Right. Then after they rehearsed a couple of times, you took the gun back from Mr. Post and kept it where?"

Mr. McCann shook his head. "By the time I got back onto the set, Post had stormed off with the gun. I went straight to Forbes because I didn't want Post breaking procedure and the heat coming back on me. But Forbes said better to leave him alone for his break. Apparently, he was in a mood. *Actors.*"

"As a firearms expert, what do you do aside from working in film?" Rosa asked.

"Oh, just film these days. Believe me, they keep me busy and pay for rentals when they use my stuff. That makes working with the odd belligerent actor more than worth it."

Miguel nodded and marked something in his notebook. "You're saying Mr. Post kept the revolver with him in his trailer throughout the break and then brought it back to set with him when they were ready to film?"

Mr. McCann nodded, but Rosa corrected him. "He forgot to bring it from his trailer, didn't he?"

The props master glanced at Rosa for the first time, paused on her for only a second, and then looked back to Miguel. "Right, yeah. The guy was too pigheaded to give it back like he was supposed to, and then he forgets it? I had to make a sprint to his trailer and back, or I'd be the one in trouble with the brass for it."

"You went straight to Mr. Post's trailer and back?" Miguel asked, noting it.

"Yes, sir."

"He was back with it very quickly," Rosa confirmed. "Less than a minute, I'd say."

"And then, after Scott collapsed, Mr. McCann," Miguel started. "You were the person to retrieve the gun from Mr. Post again?"

"Retrieve?" Mr. McCann let out a humorless laugh. "It's a one-hundred-dollar gun, and the guy dropped it on my props cart like it was a piece of trash."

"If I'm not mistaken, it's a Colt Single Action revolver," Rosa said. "An army revolver; *the peacekeeper,* they call it." She looked at Miguel, "A classic."

Both men stared at her in surprise. Even though, in England, most police officers only had basic firearm training, Rosa was familiar with revolvers. Her mother, having been raised in America, thought it important that she learn about weapons, and her father agreed. Rosa had spent many a happy afternoon in the country with her parents as they instructed her in the use of firearms and engaged her in hours of target practice until she became a crack shot. She had developed a keen interest in weaponry and over time took it upon herself to get very comfortable with different types of revolvers and studied their history. It made it easier to understand forensic ballistic reports and to know the limitations and strengths of a weapon that a fugitive might be carrying.

Rosa's recently purchased snub-nosed Smith & Wesson Colt Cobra, otherwise known as a .38 special, was meant for her protection. Kept in whatever purse she carried, the gun was with her most of the time.

"I'm sorry," Mr. McCann said, looking at her and shaking his head. "Who did you say you were again?"

Before Rosa could open her mouth, Miguel answered. "Miss Rosa Reed, formerly of the London Metropolitan Police and now a private detective here in Santa Bonita. She consults with the Santa Bonita Police on occasion."

Mr. McCann furrowed his eyebrows. "Weren't you a saloon gal?"

Rosa groaned inwardly. "I had some free time."

"Mr. McCann, is Miss Reed right about the gun?" Miguel held his pen to his notepad.

"Yeah, that's right." He finally looked back at Miguel. "Forbes wanted the peacekeeper because of its distinctive look. It's an old-fashioned revolver, and, like I mentioned before, it fits right in with the time period of this movie. The peacekeeper was a very popular gun back then.

Crossing his arms, which wrinkled his cotton shirt at the elbows, Mr. McCann continued, "The gun is almost brand new, though. The Colt Company reissued it last year, and I bought one right away when I heard about it. It's a .44 caliber. The real bullet would pack quite a punch." He adjusted his hat, tipping it to the right. "I checked the pistol before rehearsal, and it was loaded with a blank. No bullet, just gunpowder. I made sure of it. I didn't have the gun in my hands again until I ran back to Post's trailer to fetch it."

"And then again, when Mr. Post dropped it onto your props cart after filming the scene?" Miguel said.

Mr. McCann shook his head. "No, Mr. Forbes took the thing. I never got a look at it again."

Miguel glanced at Rosa, and the expression on his face was clear. *Are you sure you want to take this case? Nicholas Post is the obvious suspect here.*

13

Considerably posher than the others just visited, Nicholas Post's trailer was next on their list. A full-sized sofa ran along one side of the trailer, and Nicholas Post made a little effort to hide that he was resting on it when Rosa and Miguel knocked and entered.

"Ah, Miss Reed," he said, pulling himself into a seated position, "I expected you, but the detective coming along is a surprise."

"We're both after the same thing, Mr. Post," Rosa explained. "Finding the killer, and, of course, clearing your name." She removed the paperwork from her purse, unfolded it, and laid it on the small table. "I have nothing to lose by working closely with the police, but if you'd rather not engage me, I'd understand."

"Oh, don't go jumping to conclusions, Miss Reed. I

suspect you have means at your disposal that the police department doesn't have. Rules and such."

"I am not known for breaking the rules, Mr. Post."

Mr. Post shot a look at Miguel and then back at Rosa. "Uh-huh." Rosa didn't like the conspiratorial inference in his tone. He then picked up the contract, read it rather quickly in Rosa's estimation, then patting his pocket for a pen and finding one, signed his name with a flourish.

Rosa collected the papers and studied the signature. "Nikolai Postovik?"

Mr. Post lifted a shoulder. "Nicholas Post is a stage name. Everyone wants to sound English, don't they, Miss Reed? It's better for business."

"I am English."

"Well, bully for you." He winked at her.

Rosa forced herself not to roll her eyes. For a grown man, Mr. Post's behavior could be rather childish.

"Do you mind if Detective Belmonte and I ask a few questions?" Rosa said. "I guarantee that I intend to learn what I can to accomplish what you hired me to do."

Mr. Post waved a hand. "I hope you don't mind if I smoke."

A well-used ashtray and a half-empty pack of cigarettes sat on the table. Mr. Post found a lighter and lit a cigarette.

"You've fired guns before?" Rosa asked. "In other films?"

Nicholas Post didn't seem to want to answer this. Rosa sensed it was a point of ego more than anything, so she pushed a little harder. "Have you ever actually fired a gun in another film, Mr. Post?"

"Of course, I've fired a gun. Shooting is practically an American pastime. I suppose you have a different experience with the general public in England not having access to guns."

"Most men in Britain have fired a gun before. We did have two wars, you know." She sighed, "It's a simple question, Mr. Post." Why did he instinctively attack her? She was on his side.

"So, working with Dennis McCann wasn't your first opportunity of dealing with a firearms' expert on a movie set?" she pressed.

"No. I'd been through the rundown plenty of times. Nothing to learn from that upstart. The guy looks like he spends all day surfing, not studying up on weapons. I showed him I could shoot off six rounds of blanks, and we were done."

"What did you think of Scott Huntington?" Miguel asked. "Had the two of you worked together before?"

"Not much and yes." Mr. Post snuffed out the butt of his cigarette. "Huntington was a great stuntman, I'll give him that, but he was a lousy actor. It was annoying to watch how Forbes bent over backward to make the guy happy. Even if you held a gun to his head and demanded he smile, Huntington couldn't."

Rosa held in the gasp that threatened.

Mr. Post had the decency to look sheepish. "Oops—gun to his head—bad choice of words. See here, I didn't want the guy dead, just off my movie. And for God's sake, I wouldn't have shot him with everyone watching? Are you kidding me?"

"Who do you think wanted to see Scott Huntington dead?" Rosa asked.

Mr. Post shrugged. "I can't think of anyone who would *kill* him, but no one wanted him on the film though. Even Forbes."

Rosa cocked her head slightly. "But didn't Frederick Forbes hire him?"

"Yeah, but I told him it would ruin both of our reputations. Maybe this was Forbes' solution to cut his losses—he could have had any of his employees put a real bullet in the gun, and no one would ever put the blame on Frederick Forbes, not if they ever wanted to work in this business again," he said.

Rosa thought it rather convenient of her client to cast suspicion on the director, but she couldn't rule out assassination. The killer might've been a hired gunman.

Miguel rubbed his chin, then asked, "Why did you ask to use the gun during rehearsal? It's my understanding that firearms on set during that time wasn't standard procedure."

Mr. Post crossed his arms, his shirtsleeves tightening around well-formed biceps. "I'm an actor, Detective. I need proper props to draw out my best performance."

"But it was the rehearsal, not the final shoot," Miguel said.

"It's a rehearsal *for* the final shoot. I want to know that I can bring the performance needed. It's how I work. Not a biggie."

"And yet you forgot it in your trailer," Miguel said. "I'd think that something that important to your work would be at the top of your mind."

Mr. Post let his gaze linger on Rosa. "She knows why I forgot. You saw me, Miss Reed, I know you did."

Miguel turned his head sharply to stare at Rosa. Like a tidal wave heading to shore, Rosa knew the catastrophe she'd hoped to avoid was about to crash. Her face grew warm with dread.

"What did you see, Rosa?"

She hurried to explain the circumstances. "I was looking for the loo, the honey wagon."

"The toilets," Mr. Post explained smugly.

"So?" Miguel said, confusion on his face. "What did you see that could defend Mr. Post?"

"He was with someone in her trailer. I saw them come out."

"Who was he with?"

Mr. Post answered for her. "My lovely leading lady. Miss Winters. You can ask her."

As if he'd spent a year in the sun, Miguel's milky-coffee-brown skin instantly darkened, his humiliation coming off like waves. His dark eyes pierced Rosa. "You knew this?"

Rosa swallowed dryly, but words wouldn't form. She simply nodded.

Nicholas Post sat up. "Hey, what's going on? No wait, don't tell me Miss Winters was spoken for already." He hitched a thumb in Miguel's direction. "By you?"

"Excuse me," Miguel said, his voice choked with anger. He then turned, stormed out of the trailer, and slammed the door so hard that the trailer shook as if a California earthquake had hit.

In a way, Rosa thought, *one had.*

14

"Miguel!"

The trailers were lined up in a row with enough space in between for a person to disappear. Rosa ran the length of Nicholas Post's trailer, nearly turning an ankle on her shoe. When she had chosen shoes with short-pointed "kitten" heels to go with her outfit that morning, she'd hardly expected to be dashing about. She turned at the first break, rounded the back, and took the next turn past a neighboring trailer as she searched for Miguel in the maze.

"Miguel?"

Rosa quieted herself and listened. There didn't seem to be anyone else nearby. Besides her breath, all she could hear were birds chirping and a breeze blowing through a nearby Mexican elderberry tree, making a soft flute sound. Then came a pounding against tin as if a man was pounding the side of a trailer with his fist.

Rosa followed the sound and found Miguel standing in the short space between two trailers, his fists tight at his side. His hat lay on the grass where it had fallen off his head. Rosa bent down to pick it up.

Miguel's jaw was tight, and his eyes awash with emotional torment. The last time she'd seen him this way was eleven years earlier, and his torment had been directed at her. He'd professed his love, and she had in return, but it hadn't been enough to save them.

Rosa's heart pinched with a special pain, knowing that Miguel's heart could be torn apart by a woman other than herself. That he'd fallen in love again, something Rosa hadn't been able to do.

The way he stared at her with accusation in his eyes slew her, and she dropped her gaze to his hat in her hands.

"Why didn't you say something?"

Rosa looked up. "It's not that easy, Miguel. And I didn't see them do anything."

"You still should've told me. You could have called me or something."

He was right. Beyond personal reasons, it was information that could've been and had proved to be important to the case, but his anger was misdirected, and it made her mad. She attacked back.

"If you'd seen Larry with someone, would you have told me?"

Miguel jerked at the mention of Larry's name, his eyes narrowing. "Yes."

"What if I had cheated on Larry? Would you have told him?"

"Probably not."

"Why?"

"Because I don't care about Larry, Rosa."

Rosa's breath hitched. The inference was that Miguel still cared about her, and if she felt the same way about him, she would've told him about Charlene.

"I'm sorry, Miguel. I wanted to tell you. You had the right to know."

Miguel released a long, shaky breath of pent up air. "Just forget about it. It's not your fault that Charlene's a floozy. It's not like I didn't know she had it in her." He ran a hand through his dark hair then reached out a hand for his hat.

Rosa passed it to him.

"I should go talk to her," he said. "If she cheated with Post, who's to say she wouldn't lie to protect him."

"Why don't you wait a bit on that," Rosa suggested. "I think we should see Mr. Forbes and ask him to show us the film he shot when Mr. Huntington died."

"Yes, good idea," Miguel said. As if to clear his head, he sniffed sharply. His demeanor changed from a man who'd been betrayed to a professional with a job to do. "Now, which way to his trailer?"

Rosa had gotten a little discombobulated, the view from the back of the trailers being unfamiliar. "Let's go back to the main road," she said. "We'll get our bearings there."

Rosa resisted the urge to take Miguel by the hand, but instead, led the way back to the front of the trailer park, her back to Miguel and her eyes averted —her attempt to give him time to collect himself further. A personal betrayal like that wasn't something one just shut off in a few moments. Miguel had planned to marry Charlene, and who knew for sure that he still wouldn't. Charlene Winters was not only beautiful, but she could be charming and even persuasive.

Not until they reached the director's trailer did Rosa turn to Miguel. "Are you ready?"

"As I'll ever be."

The main door was open, so Rosa expected someone to be inside when she knocked on the screen. "Hello? Mr. Forbes?"

A gruff voice answered, "Come in!"

"Yeah, yeah, I'll call you when I'm back in LA." The director had a telephone wired to his trailer, and he held it up against his loose jowls. "Yeah, soon. Just waiting for the police to give their okay. They're here now, so maybe today. I'll let ya know. Just keep that project open for me, will ya?"

He let the receiver land on its cradle with a clang then tented his fingers together. "Good news?"

Miguel answered, "Not yet, I'm afraid."

The director sighed then pulled a cigar out of his pocket. "I'm not celebratin' anythin'. Just no sense waitin' for somethin' to cheer about and let these Cubans go to waste, ya know what I'm sayin'?"

He clipped the end of the cigar and lit it, the end glowing red as he puffed. Soon the small space smelled of sweet tobacco.

"What do you want?"

He hadn't invited them to sit, so Rosa and Miguel stayed standing. She doubted if they'd be long.

"We just have a few more questions for you. It shouldn't take long," Miguel said. "Would you be willing to show the film you took yesterday?"

"The dailies?" Mr. Forbes' gaze darted from Miguel to Rosa, who nodded. "We'd be obliged."

"I can see I don't exactly have a choice. There are only a few minutes from that day. I'll need to set up a projector in a dark room."

"There's a restaurant near the set," Rosa said. "You could set up there. It's darker than a tent."

"Ah, Bernall's, sure. I'll need some time to check on the tape. John Salvatore's getting it developed."

"Where is John Salvatore?" Rosa asked. He was on her list of crew members to question, but she hadn't seen him on site since the shoot the day before.

Mr. Forbes took a long drag of his cigar. "You got me. I haven't seen the man all day. He's a strange one, hard to get to know. Does his job but aloof if you know what I mean. Hasn't meshed well with the crew." He looked up at Miguel. "I thought the cops told everyone to stay put."

"We did," Miguel said. "Mr. Salvatore isn't in his trailer?"

"Not that I know of."

Rosa did a mental check of her impressions of John Salvatore, and they lined up with what Mr. Forbes said. Aloof would be one word she would use as well. Her impression was that the AD liked his job but didn't like people so much, but maybe there was more to it. She faced Miguel.

"We have to find Mr. Salvatore."

15

The afternoon had snuck up on them, and Miguel thought it would be good to take a break for lunch.

"I suppose we should," Rosa said. She didn't have much of an appetite, but it would be good to keep her strength up.

They decided on a Mexican café just at the edge of the *Quick Strike* compound where "Hollywood" ended, and the real world began. Crew members touched up the paint on facades, cleaned sidewalks and streets, and adjusted film equipment. One film camera looked like it had been dismantled and was now being put back together.

Would the film studio cancel the shoot, given the murder and the negative press it would inevitably generate? Rosa wondered. At some point, this area of

Santa Bonita would be resuming normal business, and when that happened, any clues left on the set would be gone forever. A growing sense of urgency bloomed in Rosa's belly. She and Miguel needed to find their break —that *one* significant clue that, like a house of cards, would bring everything down around the murderer's ears.

As they walked inside to look for a place to sit, they passed a woman at a table. She wore a nametag that read "Pam Vickers". *Where do I know that name from?* Rosa settled on that thought until she remembered the name from her conversation with Mary Williamson. Pam Vickers was the one who'd had an affair with Scott Huntington.

She whispered from the side of her mouth at Miguel. "I believe that's Miss Pam Vickers, one of the hairdressers on set. We need to talk to her. She was involved with Scott Huntington."

Believing in serendipity, Rosa smiled and immediately approached. "Miss Vickers? I'm Rosa Reed, one of the extras."

The hairdresser's deeply dark eyebrows raised in recognition. "Saloon girl number two! From London!" She smiled. "One of the other makeup ladies pointed you out to me. Not often we get an extra from London."

Rosa laughed. "No, I imagine not. This is Detective Belmonte, the lead officer on the Scott Huntington case. I work as a private investigator and sometimes consult with the police. Do you mind if we join you?"

All the cheer in Miss Vickers' round face evaporated. "By all means."

Rosa and Miguel slid into the booth opposite Miss Vickers who seemed to be unabashedly enjoying a treat of sugar-coated churros.

"I need to warn you; I am a talker," she said as she took another bite. She pronounced it *tawk-uh*. "Comes with the job, you know. We hairdressers like to gossip and talk away the day."

"You seem to enjoy your job," Rosa said.

"It's interesting. Every day is different. I guess you can say the same about your profession, right, Miss Reed? Funny, I'd never peg you as a PI."

"Most people don't, which, as a rule, works in my favor."

A young waitress arrived and took Rosa and Miguel's orders.

Miss Vickers pushed her empty plate to the side and sipped her coffee. Rosa couldn't think of a better time to just jump in. She shot Miguel a glance before saying, "I understand that you and Scott Huntington were in a relationship until not too long ago?"

"Hmph. Now you have hit on a subject I am not

eager to talk about." She patted sugar off her pouty lips and took another sip of coffee.

"I understand it ended badly?"

"Wow, you are good at your job. Not bad for arriving just yesterday as an extra. Like I said, I suddenly don't feel like talkin'."

Miguel cleared his throat. "It's my place to remind you, Miss Vickers, that this is a murder investigation. If you prefer to take it to the precinct, I can arrange that."

Pam Vickers shook her head. "Turning the screws, eh? Fine." She scowled. "Now I'm a polite lady, so I am not gonna swear here in this fine establishment. She leaned in closer and lowered her voice. "But Scott Huntington was a..." She paused and looked up as if searching for the right word ". . . rhymes with *glass bowl*."

"That bad?"

"He was terrible."

Miss Vickers sighed with unhappy reminiscing. "Yeah, we were a thing for a while. I should have known better because of his bad reputation with the ladies. In an instant, he decided he was done with me and broke things off in front of everybody. It was humiliating. I cried for a week." She looked away and then back at Rosa. "So yeah, you'll have to forgive me if I am not heartbroken about his death. Sounds cold, but there ya go." She lifted her coffee cup, frowned when realizing it was empty, then pushed it aside. "I'm done talking about that, sorry."

"Do you live in LA?" Miguel asked.

"Uh-huh."

"Any family?"

"Just a brother." Pam Vickers' eyes grew bright with pride. "Hal's a decorated war hero. He was a designated marksman on D-Day on Omaha Beach, among other things."

A hired gunman?

"Sounds like an amazing man," Rosa said. "Does he ever visit you on set?"

Miss Vickers lifted a shoulder. "Yeah, sometimes."

"Miss Vickers," Miguel started. "What you were doing between rehearsal breaks yesterday morning?"

She thought for a moment. "I went looking for Nicholas Post. It's my job to make sure his hair is okay. That means I have to follow him around a lot. Not the most pleasant part of my role here."

Rosa lowered her voice as if to conspire. "He's a bit of a wolf, isn't he?"

"I think you British people would use the word *cad*, wouldn't you?"

Rosa had to chuckle. "Very good!"

"Anyways, I couldn't find him. He was supposed to be in his trailer where I could fix his *precious* blond locks." She blinked rapidly, "But he wasn't there."

"Did you look in his trailer?" Miguel asked.

"I peeked in, yeah."

"What about the revolver," Rosa said. "Did you see it there?"

"Nope. I didn't see it. Besides, I wouldn't stick around the trailer too long in case I got seen by Mary Williamson. She's very, um, protective of him."

"She takes her job seriously, I suppose," Rosa said.

"Oh, I think she takes it a few steps too far sometimes. Honestly. Makeup and hair people have had run-ins with her. She scolds them like a schoolteacher if she thinks his hair or makeup wasn't done just right."

The waitress arrived with Rosa and Miguel's orders of tacos and coca cola on one large tray.

Miss Vickers gathered her purse and shifted toward the end of the booth. "It's okay if I go now, right?"

Miguel lowered his chin. "Just don't leave Santa Bonita for the time being."

"How long?" the hairdresser whined. "I've got things to do. Hey, I'm not a suspect, am I?"

Rosa gave the lady a reassuring look. "You have nothing to be concerned about if your hands are clean."

Pam Vickers smiled and held up her palms toward Rosa while wiggling her fingers. "Nothing but sugar and fried dough here, m'lady."

16

Pam Vickers' sudden departure made the space between Rosa and Miguel, seated next to each other in the booth, feel suddenly too intimate. Despite the aromatic smells of salsa and cilantro, Rosa was intensely caught up in the scent of Miguel's musky aftershave. Her pencil skirt didn't provide the natural barrier between their legs that her crinoline skirts would.

She muttered, "Um, I think I'll move to the other side."

Rosa was just about to slide out of the booth when Detective Sanchez barreled in through the doors.

"Found ya!" he said with a look of victory on his face. He landed his rumpled self on the opposite booth seat and adjusted his crooked tie. "I've been up and down the set, and if it hadn't been for me being lucky enough to run into Miss Vickers, I'd still be looking, I reckon." He lifted a beefy arm, and his suit jacket spread open to reveal a shirt that had been buttoned incorrectly.

"Miss," he called out. His eyes focused on Rosa and Miguel's plates for a second before he continued. "I'll have what they're having, times two."

"So, you found me?" Miguel said. "What do you have to report?"

"We found a bullet casing. Must've got kicked about in that dirt the production hauled in."

"Why do you say that?" Rosa asked.

"It wasn't anywhere near where you'd expect it to be if it came from the prop gun. One of our guys found it under a horse trough when the crew was repainting it. Ballistics has it now."

Miguel dug into his taco, but Rosa couldn't stop thinking about what Detective Sanchez had said. "What if it wasn't from the prop gun?" she said.

Miguel paused mid-bite. "What are you suggesting?"

"Perhaps there was a second gun on set yesterday. Anyone who knew the script, or for that matter, had sat through the numerous rehearsals, would know exactly when the prop gun would be fired."

"You think someone else took a shot at the same time Post pulled the trigger?"

"It's possible."

"Weren't there a lot of people on set?" Detective Sanchez said. "Someone would've seen a second shooter."

"There were a lot of people," Rosa admitted, "but we were all looking at the action, not the people around us. I think it would be possible. Especially if the second gun had a suppressor on it."

"It's a theory worth investigating," Miguel said. "I definitely want to see those dailies now."

Detective Sanchez's tacos arrived. Moments of silence ticked away as he lapped up taco juice as it dripped from the shell and slurped his soda.

Rosa dabbed at her lips with a napkin then said, "What do we know for certain?" She resisted the urge to retrieve her notebook from her purse, not wanting grease stains on the pages.

"Post called for the gun in rehearsal even though it's not standard practice," Detective Sanchez said. "I find that highly peculiar."

"However, the prop gun came from Dennis McCann's personal collection."

"Also, highly peculiar." Detective Sanchez put a fist to his mouth, apparently to hold in a belch. "Pardon me."

"McCann claims Post is well acquainted with the Colt .44, though Post denies knowing much about guns," Miguel said. He turned his neck to face Rosa. "Doesn't look too good for your client."

"Nicholas Post *forgot*. . ." Detective Sanchez used two fingers of both hands to mimic quotation marks around the words, "the prop gun in his trailer."

Rosa couldn't stop herself from coming to her client's defense. "It was Mr. McCann who sprinted back to get it."

"After Forbes told him to," Miguel said.

"It could've been a crime of opportunity," Rosa said, though she didn't believe it herself.

Detective Sanchez shrugged a thick shoulder. "If Mr. Post planned to kill Scott Huntington in that fashion, why pretend to forget the gun?"

"So he could blame the switch up on someone else," Miguel said. "As long as he can claim he was away from the gun for any length of time, there's room for someone else to go into his trailer and make the switch."

"Where was Post, anyway?" Sanchez said. He dropped his napkin onto his empty plate with a flourish. "What's his alibi?"

Rosa felt Miguel stiffen. She wasn't about to rat out his fiancée to his colleague, but the information was important, and she waited for Miguel to explain.

A tense silence filled the booth.

"*What?*" Detective Sanchez said. "What am I

missing?"

Rosa waited for Miguel to do the right thing, but he stunned her by saying, "Nothing. It's nothing. Let's go see if Forbes is ready with his film."

The film projector was set up in the back room of a restaurant Rosa had suggested earlier. On a blank wall hung a makeshift screen providing the producer with a chance to review the dailies.

"Where the devil is John Salvatore?" Mr. Forbes bellowed.

Rosa wondered the same thing. The elusive assistant director was definitely on her list of people to see next.

With a huff, the director took over the operation of the projector.

Rosa, Miguel, and Detective Sanchez sat on wooden chairs in a row on one side of the projector, waiting for the lead strips of white tape to run. The first frame showed John Salvatore's hands closing the slapper board, which listed the take, the scene, and the film roll numbers.

They watched as the camera followed Scott Huntington on his path, upending tables and knocking over boardwalk as he went.

"Now. This is camera number one, which focuses

on Scott. Camera number two will pick up Mr. Post, and we'll see those two edited together."

Suddenly the film showed Nicholas Post running onto the street and yelling. When the shot returned to Scott Huntington, Rosa was startled to see that she and Gloria were on the very edge of the shot. It seemed odd to see herself in a moving film like this. Her parents had a Kodak 8 mm film camera and had taken some film footage of her a few years ago, but it was not nearly as clear as this and not in color.

Then the shot rang out, reverberating off the buildings. Scott Huntington fell as Rosa had seen him do in person.

Rosa strained to see a clue that would lead to a break in the case or a new lead, but she could see nothing she hadn't noted when she was live on set. Although something about it bothered her, she couldn't quite put her finger on it.

They watched the footage several times. Miguel even asked Mr. Forbes to slow the film down. They watched it twice in slow motion.

Someone finally flicked the lights on, and everyone squinted momentarily as their eyes adjusted. Rosa shared a look of disappointment with Miguel. Detective Sanchez slapped his thighs for lack of something better to do.

"Well," Mr. Forbes said with a note of belligerence

in his voice. He lit up a cigar, puffed hard and then said, "I knew this would be a waste of time."

Miguel got to his feet. "Not at all. Miss Reed was there, so she had no problem imagining the events as they unfolded, but for Detective Sanchez and me, this was very enlightening."

"How so?" the director asked, looking rather stunned by Miguel's proclamation. Rosa felt similarly.

Miguel stared somberly at the director. "I have to keep some things close to my chest, for now, director."

Outside the restaurant and out of earshot of Mr. Forbes, Rosa cocked her head as she considered Miguel. "You're acting rather mysteriously."

Miguel huffed. "It's a bluff. We need the cooperation of the director, or we may lose the cooperation of the whole crew. As it is, we can't force them to stay in Santa Bonita much longer."

"We still haven't questioned Mr. Salvatore," Rosa said. "Do you think he's done a runner?"

"Maybe. Sanchez put out an all-points bulletin on the AD, in case he decides to scram."

Detective Sanchez plopped his hat back onto his head. "Got it, boss. I'm heading back to the precinct."

"I'm right behind you," Miguel said.

Detective Sanchez dipped his chin toward Rosa. "Always a pleasure, Miss Reed."

A feeling of dread soured Rosa's throat. She

couldn't ignore the obvious. "Um, about Charlene," she said gently. When she glanced up at Miguel, he kept his gaze on her.

Miguel quietly mentioned, "She wasn't in the frame when the gun went off."

"You noticed that too."

"Wouldn't be much of a cop if I didn't."

"I'm sorry, I didn't mean—" Rosa began.

"No, I'm sorry. I shouldn't have snapped at you. This isn't your fault."

"I'm sure she's innocent, I mean she has no motive that I can think of, but like everyone else on the set, you need to ask her where she was," Rosa said, because if Miguel didn't then, out of contractual obligation to Mr. Post, Rosa would have to. She might anyway as much as the thought disagreed with her.

"I know. I'll do it right now. You don't mind if I go alone?" Miguel said.

"Of course not! I'm going to check in with my client anyway."

"I'll be back at the precinct later if you need me for anything."

Rosa hated how stiff and formal she suddenly felt with Miguel. It wasn't like they were friends, but they had, at times, been friendly.

Try as she might, Rosa couldn't shake off the heaviness in her heart as she watched Miguel walk away.

17

"Mr. Post?" Rosa saw Nicholas Post napping on the couch through the screen door of his trailer. She tapped lightly on the door. "Do you have a second?"

Mr. Post opened one eye. His lip twitched at the corner as a grin formed. "Are you alone?"

"Yes."

"Then, I have all the seconds in the world." The actor pulled himself into a sitting position. "Come in, Miss Reed."

"I'm sorry to bother you," Rosa said as she stepped inside, "but the nature of my business is to inconvenience people."

"Understood." Mr. Post tapped the sofa beside him. "Why don't you come and sit over here?" His face spread into the winning smile she'd seen on movie posters.

"Thank you, but this seat is fine." Rosa sat at the small table and reached for her notebook. "I know you've been asked a lot of questions already, and some from me, but it would help me to understand factually and in order, the events leading up to the gunshot that killed Mr. Huntington."

"Shoot."

Rosa's gaze darted to the actor.

"I mean, go ahead, ask your questions."

"When you went for the rehearsal yesterday, was that the first time you'd seen the gun that day?"

"Yeah, yeah." Mr. Post leaned back and spread out his arms along the back of the sofa. "Like I said before, Dennis went over all the features, showed me that only blanks were inside, all of that."

"And what does a blank look like?" Rosa knew the answer but needed to be certain her client knew.

Mr. Post scowled. "Like a real cartridge except no bullet on the end of it."

"Do you have any access to bullets, Mr. Post? Do you own any or keep any at home or in your vehicle?"

"Please, call me Nick." He smiled broadly at her. She didn't smile back.

"I like to keep it professional."

"I don't own any guns, so why would I have

bullets?" Mr. Post stared at the small desk near Rosa, and his eyes stayed there for a long time. So long that Rosa suspected that was where he had placed the gun when he'd come back for the break. The desk was only a foot from the door. A person wouldn't have even had to step inside to retrieve it.

Rosa reached out an arm and tapped the top of the desk. "Is this where the gun sat during the break?"

"That's where I left it, and then I forgot about it. As I told you and that detective already, I was busy with my leading lady in her trailer. Have you talked to her yet?"

"Not yet."

"Hey, I ain't no private detective, but if I were trying to prove someone's innocence, I'd nail down the alibi."

"I plan to talk to Miss Winters," Rosa said, "but she's currently being interviewed by the police. "Who else could have had access to your trailer while you were gone?"

"Any number of people. Hair and makeup came by all the time. So did wardrobe, John Salvatore, Forbes. And, of course, Mary, but they would never touch the gun."

"But someone from the crew might?" Rosa asked.

Nicholas Post laughed. "Sure. Everyone wants to

touch a movie star's things. Even some of the directors I've worked with."

"You don't lock your trailer?"

"What? No one does. A pain in the rear, if you know what I mean. This ain't LA."

"One more question, Mr. Post. Did you check the cylinder when the gun was brought back to set before the filming?"

The actor shook his head. "There was no time. Because of all the mess up that Huntington had caused, Forbes was eager to shoot the scene."

From the trailer window, Rosa glimpsed movement outside. Miss Williamson was hovering, and Rosa hoped she hadn't been eavesdropping on her conversation with Mr. Post. There was no time like the present to ask the secretary a few questions.

Rosa got to her feet, slid the notebook into her purse, and stepped toward the door. "I'll let you know once I've learned anything new, Mr. Post," she said.

"Hey, you're still working for me, right?"

"Of course."

"Cause, I can't help but feel you're helping the police to pin this on me."

"Not at all, Mr. Post. But I am trusting that everything you've told me so far is the truth."

Mr. Post held out his palms, touching the flesh of his little fingers together. "Miss, I'm an open book."

"Brilliant."

Rosa stepped to the grassy ground outside, but Miss Williamson was nowhere to be seen. The door to the secretary's small trailer, however, was cracked open.

"Miss Williamson?"

Though the secretary sat at the table, pen in hand, looking busy at work, she still had her hat on, which suggested she'd not been back long.

"Oh, Miss Reed?" Miss Williamson pushed a lock of hair behind her ears. "Come in."

Though small, the travel trailer was well equipped with a small couch, which no doubt folded out into a bed, a kitchenette with a gas stove, and a small refrigerator. There was a table with two padded, cloth-covered benches. Rosa sat opposite Miss Williamson. On the table were a pile of folders, some promotional shots of Nicholas Post, and a coffee mug. Several framed pictures of Mary Williamson with Nicholas Post hung on the wall.

"Just a couple of quick questions," Rosa said, "and I'll let you get back to work. During the rehearsal break, did you go inside Mr. Post's trailer?

Miss Williamson shook her head. "I made coffee for Mr. Post."

"So, you weren't in Mr. Post's trailer at all?" Rosa asked her.

"No."

"What exactly is your job, Miss Williamson?"

This question seemed to surprise her. "Well I . . . I am Mr. Post's assistant. I make sure he has everything he needs."

"Such as?" Rosa started to write.

"Anything really. The job ranges from getting coffee to helping him schedule his appointments. I often help him pick out his wardrobe and sometimes pick up groceries for him back in LA . . . one time I helped him pick out new furniture for his house in Beverly Hills."

"You must be pretty close?"

The PA's face suddenly went red. "I . . . I have to admit, I have sometimes had to act as a sort of counselor too. As you can imagine, Nicholas has a very complicated life."

"How long have you been doing that?" Rosa kept writing.

"I guess over a year now."

"You must know how Mr. Post felt toward Scott Huntington then."

"There's a bit of rivalry there. Sure. I think that's well known. But Nicholas murdering someone . . ." She vigorously shook her head. "Well, that idea is just far beyond the realm of possibility."

"Is it?"

"Yes! People have this perception that Nicholas is a tough character, and I mean he is a very strong man, of course, but it's also true that he has a tender heart and wouldn't hurt a fly."

Recalling the suspicious words Miss Vickers had said about Miss Williamson, and how protective she was of her boss, Rosa asked, "When I talked to you earlier, you mentioned Pam Vickers?"

"*Who?*" Miss Williamson pushed wayward strands of red hair off her face. "Oh, the hair mistress. Yes, she had an affair with Scott Huntington that went badly. I told you that she might be someone to investigate."

"I did. She mentioned that you were sometimes unhappy with the way she did Mr. Post's hair."

"What a busybody! If she'd just do her job, I wouldn't have to complain." Miss Williamson paused as if in thought. "In fact, she was needed on set to do touch-ups, and do you think I could find her then? No."

Rosa made her way to the AD's trailer and raised her hand to knock on the door.

"What do you think you're doing?"

Rosa jumped at an angry voice behind her. John Salvatore.

"Mr. Salvatore! Just the person I was looking for. You're a hard man to find."

"Not when I want to be found. Who are you?"

"I'm Miss Rosa Reed of Reed Investigations."

Mr. Salvatore shook his head impatiently. "So?"

"I've been hired by Mr. Post—"

John Salvatore broke out in a loud, humorless laugh. "And what are *you* supposed to do to help him? Make him dinner? Ha! Knowing Post, he'd want you barefoot."

"Mr. Salvatore, there's no need for crudeness. I only want to ask a few questions."

John Salvatore moved in close, so close that their height difference became apparent. He was several inches taller than Rosa, and he glared down at her as though he was more than comfortable with this intimidation tactic. "Would you like to go inside?"

Rosa shifted sideways and stepped back. She couldn't help but notice how quiet the grounds were. Rosa guessed many people had probably left for the day as it was now after five.

"I'm fine out here," she said. "I'm just wondering how you ended up with this job. I understand Mr. Forbes usually works with another AD."

"Luck of the draw, I guess. Forbes needed a new AD. And I needed a job."

"Have you always worked in films?"

Mr. Salvatore chuckled. "Among other things."

"You don't sound like a California native, Mr. Salvatore."

"Neither do you, Miss Reed."

"As you can probably tell, I'm from England, and I'm going to guess that you're from *New* England. "

"You know your accents. Boston's my hometown."

"My family used to live there. It's where my mother grew up."

"How nice. Now, if we're done with this little tea social, I got work to do."

Rosa had never seen John Salvatore and Scott Huntington interact in a way that would suggest they had a history, and the AD was new to the set. Yet there was something slippery about Salvatore, and Rosa wouldn't be surprised if the man was hiding something. "Have you worked with Mr. Huntington before?"

Mr. Salvatore produced a sly grin and nodded. "Not that it's any of your business."

"What do you know about guns?"

"Why? Do you think I killed Scott Huntington?"

"I think you are on the list as a suspect. You disappeared off set when the police were looking for you. You seem antagonistic now, even though I am asking very common questions, Mr. Salvatore."

John Salvatore roughly grabbed her by the arm, just below her elbow.

"I'm done talkin' to you."

"Take your hand off of me immediately, sir!" Rosa said, her voice even, strong, and clipped.

Mr. Salvatore's grip grew firmer, his fingers hurting her arm as he tried to wrench her toward his trailer.

What Rosa did next was a reflex action, muscle memory simply took over from hours of self-defense training. It was as simple and practiced to her as putting on lipstick or tying a shoelace. She could still hear her instructor's commands as he grabbed her arm as an aggressor would do. "Constable Reed, you must go against your natural instinct to step back, and step into your opponent instead." Rosa had taken a step in and her instructor continued, tightening his grip on her wrist. "Now, whip this hand up to your face, palm flat like you're looking into a mirror. The movement will force your attacker's wrist into a frightfully painful position, forcing him to lessen his grip."

And like it had then, and many other times for Rosa while on the force, Mr. Salvatore was taken by surprise. Not only could he not keep his grip on Rosa, his wrist was bent backward. Rosa re-enforced the pressure by using her free hand to prop up Mr. Salvatore's elbow, then pivoted her hips away from him.

The AD now had his wrist and arm twisted painfully. His back and shoulder were forced toward Rosa, causing him to sink to his knees. The movement was so fast and unexpected, he had no countermove. He was completely under her control.

He groaned. "Okay, okay, I give!"

Rosa pushed him away from herself, which pitched him forward, face-first, onto the ground, and he landed with a grunt. Rosa didn't hang around to see if the AD had changed his mind about talking. She turned and ran to the main road, not stopping until she reached her Corvette.

18

Despite having overpowered Mr. Salvatore, Rosa gave in to a post-adrenaline bout of trembling, barely managing to start the engine of her car and drive away. She could have the assistant director arrested for assault and would likely have bruising on her wrist to prove her case. However, that would only be evidence that someone had held her, and not Mr. Salvatore specifically. With no witnesses, it would be an instance of "he said, she said".

Rosa turned on the radio and hummed along with Dean Martin's, "Memories are Made of This". By the time she got home, her nerves had settled and she was ready for a good night's sleep. But as she approached the front door of the Forrester mansion, she could hear a high-pitched screaming coming from inside. She flung the main doors open, dread squeezing her heart.

Looking disheveled, Clarence stepped into the hallway with deep frown lines on his face.

"What's happening?" Rosa asked.

"She's having a tantrum in the dining room. I can't get her off the floor."

Hurrying past her bewildered cousin, Rosa entered the room, empty of everyone but the little girl who stopped screaming suddenly at the sight of Rosa. Thankfully, the child appeared unharmed.

Rosa turned to Clarence. "Where is everyone?"

"Mom and Grandma are at a charity planning event, and Gloria's at an acting class,"

"I want my mama," Julie cried.

"Oh, you poor dear." Rosa bent a knee and took one of the little girl's hands. Julie weakly tried to pull it away, but she'd been thrashing and yelling for so long, all her strength had gone.

Rosa pushed a damp strand of honey-blonde hair off the little girl's reddened face. "I know what it's like to miss your mama. There was a time when I didn't see mine for a very long time."

Julie's voice came in quiet hiccups. "R . . .r . . . really?"

"Yes. But when my mother wasn't around, my Aunt Louisa—your grandma—filled in. It wasn't the same, but she loved me too, just like my mother loved me. And after a while, I was with my mum again."

Julie sniffled as Rosa picked her up off the floor. "And while your mommy's gone, Aunt Gloria, your grandmothers, and I will fill in for her in the same way, okay?"

"O-kay."

"And you know what you have that I didn't have?"

"What?"

"A daddy. Your daddy is here, and he loves you very much."

Julie suddenly turned her head to Clarence and stretched out her arms toward him.

Rosa handed Julie over to Clarence, who mouthed, "Thank you."

THE NEXT MORNING, Rosa was roused awake by Diego, who purred in her face and pressed his soft, furry cheek against hers.

"Good morning, Diego. I know, I know, you want breakfast."

Rosa sat up and stretched her arms overhead.

"You can go down without me, you know. Señora Gomez probably has your food out already."

Diego responded by climbing onto her lap and kneading her legs through her quilt. Rosa petted him along his silky flank. "That's enough, little mister. We've got work to do today."

Rosa pushed Diego off her legs and swung off the side of her bed. The morning sunlight peeked into the darkened room through cracks in the curtains and a few too many pinholes—thank you, Diego's claws.

Drawing the curtains back, Rosa took in the beautiful view of the sprawling grounds. She could see the large manicured lawn lined with swaying palm trees and off in the distance, the Pacific Ocean dotted with several ships on the horizon. The Forrester pool looked like a giant crystal because of the way sunlight glittered off its surface. Santa Bonita mornings were typically pleasant, warm enough to breakfast outside before the heat of the day hit, driving many people indoors if they were fortunate enough to have air conditioning.

Aunt Louisa and Grandma Sally were already breakfasting at the patio table with little Julie between them, her tantrum all but forgotten. Rosa had been so busy the last couple of days that she hadn't had a chance to mingle with either of the older women. She hurried through her morning routine and made a quick choice of a pair of floral-patterned capris and a white, sleeveless blouse. After spending the day before in a restricting pencil skirt, the choice felt liberating, and her feet thanked her for wearing ballet flats.

Rosa skipped down the stairs with Diego galloping along behind her. She was relieved to see not only were her Aunt Louisa, Grandma Sally, and little Julie still there but also Gloria and Clarence had joined them.

Gloria, wearing a playful poodle-printed skirt, patted the empty seat beside her. "Señora Gomez has already set a plate for you."

The housekeeper arrived with a fresh pot of coffee and a pleasant smile on her face.

"Gracias, Señora Gomez."

"De nada, Miss Rosa."

"We were just talking about you," Aunt Louisa said. She folded the newspaper she'd been perusing and crossed long, slender legs.

"Oh, what have I done?"

Gloria broke in, "Not you personally, silly, the . . ." She pointed at Julie, whose chubby cheeks were filled with Sugar Crisp cereal. Gloria whispered loudly, ". . . the *incident*. Do they know who's responsible for poor Scott Huntington's *demise*?" Gloria's eyes teared up, and careful not to smear her makeup, she dabbed at the corners with her napkin.

"The police are still investigating," Rosa said.

"Aren't you?" Clarence asked. "I thought Nicholas Post hired you?"

"He did. I'm cooperating with the police."

"I saw Scott Huntington on *The Roy Rogers Show* last year once," Grandma Sally said. "Such a pity when someone so young dies."

"Grandma?" Clarence said with a nod at Julie, who was staring at the pictures on the back of the cereal box.

"You can't protect her from all of life's unkindness," Grandma Sally said. "Dying is a fact of life. Before you know it, I'll be gone."

"Mom!" Aunt Louisa said. "Really."

"Well, it's true. No one lives forever."

Clarence brought a cigarette to his mouth and lit it. "Can we change the subject?"

"I read in *The Los Angeles Clandestine* that Nicholas Post was jealous about Scott Huntington's rising star," Gloria said, ignoring her brother, which Rosa knew was a pattern for both siblings.

Since Mr. Post was Rosa's client, she felt compelled to defend him. "It doesn't mean he did," she glanced at Julie, "what happened . . . there are a lot of possibilities."

Grandma Sally waved a withered hand in front of her face. "It's getting too hot for me, Louisa."

Aunt Louisa pushed away from the table, assisted her mother out of her chair, and guided her inside.

Clarence lifted his chin toward Gloria. "Has this experience turned you off acting?"

Gloria wrinkled her nose. "It's not as glamorous as the magazines make it out to be. A lot of waiting around, and when you're not waiting, you're being bossed around."

"I have to agree," Rosa said. And unlike a lot of young aspiring starlets, Gloria did not hold money as a motive for pursuing fame.

"But if I don't do that," Gloria pouted, "I don't know what I'll do."

Julie's little voice piped up. "You can play with me."

"Oh, sweetheart," Gloria cooed, patting Julie on the head. "That's such a good idea!" She held out her hand. "Let's go find something to do."

Gloria and Julie giggled as they left the breakfast table.

Rosa smiled and turned to Clarence. "Julie's such a lovely child."

"She is." Clarence turned away, trying to hide his emotions. "She deserves better."

Rosa placed a palm on her cousin's arm. "Julie has you, and she has all of us. And so do you."

Clarence glanced up with a glint of appreciation in his eyes. "Thanks, Rosa."

"Any time. Have you heard from Vanessa at all?"

"She promised she'd call, but so far, nothing. She swore up and down that she just needed time alone to get her head straight, but she's not—alone."

"What do you mean?"

"She's got a new fella. Santa Bonita's a small town, and our circle even smaller. News like that is juicy. I was bound to hear about it. Vanessa must've known that. I just wish she would shoot straight."

Clarence pushed away from the table, leaving Rosa to muse about things on her own. Clarence's parting words reverberated in her mind. *I just wish she would shoot straight.*

Rosa headed for the telephone in the kitchen. She had a call to make.

19

Rosa left Diego in the car, stepped out of her Corvette, and crossed the parking lot that led to Santa Bonita General Hospital. She planned to visit the morgue—not a place for a cat. The chemical smells alone... Besides, she was sure that Dr. Philpott would chase her out in an instant, even if Diego were on a leash.

She made her way down below the first floor and pushed on the steel doors to enter the morgue's office.

Larry's face lit up as the doors swung shut behind her. "Darlin', come in."

Rosa greeted him with a kiss, keeping it short, should a technician or nurse walk by. It was always important to Rosa that she appear professional, but the added tension of Larry's recent invitation for her to follow him to Texas hovered invisibly between them.

"Have a seat," Larry reached over to a padded chair sitting against the white wall of the morgue waiting room and slid it over to face another one which he then sat down on.

"Your timin' is great," Larry said. "We just finished up the postmortem."

"What did you learn?"

"Mr. Huntington was in perfect health. If it weren't for that bullet hole, I suspect he would've lived a right long life."

Just as he finished the sentence, the jovial figure of Dr. Philpott entered the room from a steel door on the other side of the morgue. He slid his rubber gloves off and placed them on the counter before walking over to Rosa.

"Well, Miss Reed. Good to see you again." He took both her hands in his. Though Rosa had only been in Santa Bonita a short time, she already knew Dr. Melvin Philpott well. Her relationship with the tall, spectacled, middle-aged man was quite cordial, considering Rosa had once investigated his wife, Shirley, for murder. That was when Rosa had first arrived and had immediately gotten involved with a murder case revolving around a charity that Mrs. Philpott was involved with.

She had been cleared of any wrongdoing in that case. Still, for a while, the tension between Santa Bonita's chief medical examiner and the newly arrived British policewoman had been uncomfortable. Fortunately for all involved, Melvin Philpott was a congenial man by nature, and, with the help of Miguel, the good doctor's attitude toward Rosa had soon softened.

"Larry tells me you are investigating this case as well. Did he tell you? We just finished the examination."

"Yes, he did. What can you tell me? Specifically, I would like to know if you found anything odd about the bullet hole," Rosa said. Clarence's inadvertent comment about shooting straight had caused Rosa to think about the angle of the wound.

"I think so, but I'll let Larry fill you in. I have a few phone calls to make." Dr. Philpott smiled at them both and disappeared into his office.

"I used a wooden dowel rod the same circumference as the wound," Larry said. "C'mon, you can see for yourself."

Rosa followed Larry into the sanitized postmortem operation theater where the ashen body of Scott Huntington lay on a stainless-steel slab, a sheet covering his body up to the ribcage where the neatly sewn Y incision was exposed. A two-foot-long dowel inserted into the single gunshot wound stuck out at an angle.

"If you follow the projection of the angle . . ." He pointed at the end of the dowel. "The shooter had to be standin' at least eight feet or one floor higher than ground level."

"It couldn't have come from the prop gun!" Rosa looked at Larry.

"Not if the shooter was standin' on the ground where Mr. Huntington was."

Rosa's mind went back to the image of Scott Huntington on the film footage they had watched in the restaurant. "Of course!" she snapped her fingers. "That's what niggled me when we were watching the dailies yesterday."

"Dailies?" Larry's face showed puzzlement.

"The film clips taken on any given day are called the dailies. I couldn't quite place it, but now I see it. Scott Huntington fell slightly sideways when he was shot—it wasn't much, hardly noticeable really. Still, you would expect he would have immediately fallen forward after being shot in the back. A bullet that size has a bit of a pushing effect when it hits a body."

"Correct. The bigger the bullet, the more the velocity has an impact on a stationary body."

Rosa felt a sudden sense of warm satisfaction. She had proof that her client was innocent. "There's no way the bullet could've come from Mr. Post's gun," Rosa repeated the assertion.

"Not at all."

The question was, where exactly had the shooter

been standing?

"Thank you, Larry," Rosa said. "I need to get to the movie set and figure this out, but first, I'll call into the precinct to let Miguel know."

"I've already phoned in my findings, so you can head over to the set directly if you want."

"Oh, okay."

Rosa wasn't sure if Larry was subtly trying to dissuade her from seeing Miguel, but why would he? He didn't know about Rosa and Miguel's past.

Did he?

Rosa had lived in Santa Bonita for three months—long enough that the casual rancher style of the Santa Bonita Police building no longer brought images to mind of the stark difference between it and the much more formal establishment of Scotland Yard. She had now gotten used to the swaying palm trees and the curated flower beds lining the cemented walkway, even though they didn't evoke the feeling of discipline and law enforcement.

The receptionist was also used to seeing Rosa and waved her through with a smile.

"Where's Deputy Diego?" said the portly woman behind the counter, smiling.

"Cat in a bag." Rosa raised her satchel as she

breezed past. Diego was fast asleep at the bottom, hidden from view.

Miguel was in his office, scribbling on pages at his desk, no doubt dealing with the notorious *paperwork* police around the globe dreaded. That was one part of Rosa's old job with the Metropolitan Police that she didn't miss.

"Howdy, Rosa," Miguel said when he spotted her. "I got the call from Dr. Rayburn. I assume that's why you're here?"

"It is. The autopsy finds put my client in the clear, wouldn't you agree?"

"Yes, congratulations. Your work is done."

Rosa felt the smile slip off her face. She should've known that Miguel would push her aside. Even though she'd officially been working for Mr. Post, Miguel had introduced her as a Santa Bonita Police consultant. She wouldn't rest now until the killer was found.

Ignoring Miguel's less than subtle dismissal, Rosa took a seat in one of the empty wooden chairs facing his desk. The long strap of her purse stretched in an angle from shoulder to hip. The satchel hanging from her arm was open, and Diego's face poked out of it.

Miguel's shoulders softened when he spotted the kitten's cute furry face. "I see you brought Deputy Diego along. A little late in the game, huh?"

"Well, the killer is still out there."

A dimple appeared. "And you think *he* can help?"

"No, but maybe I can. I was just at the set. There's a cafe behind and slightly to the right of where Scott Huntington was standing when he was shot. The building was open all day. On the upper floor, windows can be opened to the street below. It is unlikely crew or extras would have been up there since the exteriors were covered with facades. It's possible, if not probable, the shot came from there. The casing your men found was near the horse trough located in front of the café."

"If all this is true..." He let the thought go unfinished.

"Then all this time, we've been focusing on who might have had access to the prop gun in Nicholas Post's trailer! A clever misdirection."

"A rabbit trail," Miguel said.

"A wild goose chase."

Miguel shook his pencil at her. "A snipe hunt."

Rosa lifted her chin. "A bootless errand."

Miguel dropped his pencil on the desk and stared at her. "Really? *Bootless*?"

Rosa shrugged at her propensity for nugatory and archaic trivia, and changed the subject. "Have you had a chance to question John Salvatore yet?"

Miguel shook his head. "The assistant director appears to be a chameleon."

"I had an encounter with him yesterday."

"An encounter? And you're only telling me this now?"

Rosa remembered the emotional distress little Julie had been in.

"I meant to ring you, but I got distracted by circumstances at home."

"Everything all right?"

"Clarence's wife, Vanessa, dropped off their little girl, Julie, and then disappeared."

"Disappeared?"

"Not in a suspicious way." At least Rosa hoped not. "She was emotionally distraught and just left. Julie's had a hard time as a result."

Miguel glanced away. "I'm sorry."

Rosa ducked her chin. Clarence wasn't the only one suffering from a broken relationship.

"Back to Salvatore," Miguel said. "What happened?"

"Though Mr. Salvatore wanted us to believe otherwise, he and Mr. Huntington were acquainted. When I suggested that Mr. Salvatore purposely shielded the nature of his relationship with Mr. Huntington, he became, er, unreasonably irritated." Rosa couldn't see the benefit of telling Miguel about the physical altercation. It would only result in a scolding which she, quite frankly, could do without.

Miguel tapped a note on his desk with the tip of his fountain pen. "The movie industry is small. Everyone knows everyone, I suspect."

"Yet no one had heard of Mr. Salvatore before he started on this movie," Rosa said.

Detective Sanchez strolled in, a folder under his arm. His usual cigarette was balanced between his lips. "Hey, Miss Reed."

"Hello, Detective."

Detective Sanchez glanced at the open satchel and nodded at Diego, a twinkle playing in the detective's eyes. "Hi, cat." Then he added to Miguel and Rosa, "Did I hear you talking about Salvatore?"

Miguel rubbed the stubble on his chin. "Uh-huh."

"Turns out John Salvatore *is* a shady character. Your hunch, Mick, to call Boston police was a good one." He dropped the folder on Miguel's desk. "He is otherwise known as *Johnny Shooter*."

Rosa cocked her head. "Interesting name."

"Looks like he works for the New England mafia. More specifically, for Saul Patriarchi, from the Patriarchi family. Turns out, '*Johnny Shooter*' is one of his main enforcers."

"Enforcer?" Rosa said. "As in hired assassin?"

"Let's just say ole Johnny has shooting talents that go beyond film on movie sets."

"Now, isn't that nice," Miguel remarked.

"There's more. I did some digging around with regards to *Quick Strike*. The movie production company that is producing the film is called East Shore Productions, and here's a kicker; ESP is owned by none other than Gio Patriarchi, brother to Saul Patriarchi."

Miguel whistled and shared a look with Rosa. "All in the family, huh?"

"John Salvatore got the job on the set because the guy they had for the job had an accident."

"How convenient," Miguel said. "And I bet John Salvatore didn't plan to stay on the job very long."

Detective Sanchez pulled up the empty chair beside Rosa and reached thick fingers over to Diego, giving him a friendly pat on the head. "You're gonna love this." He pointed at the folder again. "Last year, Scott Huntington was a stuntman in a production that was shot on location in Boston."

"Mr. Salvatore admitted to me that he and Mr. Huntington had worked together before," Rosa said. "I think I saw that movie in the cinema a few nights ago."

Detective Sanchez pulled his cigarette out with two fingers and blew smoke out of the side of his mouth, something Rosa had seen him do countless times. "One of the extras was a young lady named Phyllis. Phyllis Patriarchi, the daughter of Saul Patriarchi. But here is the real punchline of the day—according to the industry rumor mill, Scott Huntington got Phyllis Patriarchi pregnant and then broke up with her on the last day of filming."

A moment of silence blanketed the room as those words hung in the air. As if Miguel had connected the dots, he stared at Detective Sanchez and muttered, "Find Salvatore and bring him in for questioning."

Rosa, with Diego in the satchel, shared a ride with Miguel in his unmarked police car back to Tiendas de Pueblo. Most restaurants and shops closed during the shoot had reopened. Dozens of people roamed the square, and it seemed like things were back to normal where the last scene had been set up—although the production trucks and trailers were still parked at the end of the square.

Walking along the street, Rosa paused on the X where Scott Huntington had stood when he'd been shot. She replayed the moment. Pointing to an empty patio table off to the left of the square, she said, "Gloria and I stood over there, close enough to be caught in the frame. Mr. Post was about twenty feet straight ahead. Behind him, were Mr. Forbes and the cameraman."

"What about John Salvatore?" Miguel asked.

"I don't know. I was focused on the scene. He was out of my peripheral vision. So was—" Rosa shot Miguel an awkward glance.

He filled in the blanks. "So was Charlene."

"Yes. In the scene before, Mr. Post's and her characters had words, and her character stormed away."

Heading toward the *Santa Kafeina* coffee shop, Rosa lugged her satchel containing Diego inside. Miguel stepped in behind her. The place was about half-full of patrons, with the strong smell of rich coffee permeating the air.

A young lady with dark hair tucked under a white cap stood behind the counter as Rosa and Miguel approached. The name tag attached to her uniform read *Francisca*.

"Excuse me," Rosa said. "Were you closed during the film shoot?"

The girl nodded. "But the doors were left open. The director paid us to keep the restrooms available. Just for the main actors and himself."

"Was anyone on site?" Miguel asked.

"Just me off and on. Someone had to keep an eye on things, and my boss wasn't interested in hanging around. I didn't mind, I mean, I wanted to see Nicholas Post in the flesh so badly! What a dreamboat! It was the best day of my life."

Rosa bit her cheek to keep from smirking. "Were you here the whole time?"

"No, I went out to watch the action during rehearsal and stuff."

"So, someone could have come in without you knowing," Miguel said.

"I guess, but why would they? And if they did, there's nothing in here to steal."

Miguel pointed at the set of stairs. "What's up there?"

"In the front, facing the street, is overflow seating. The rooms at the back are offices."

Rosa and Miguel thanked Francisca then climbed the stairs. First, they entered a room, empty but for a few tables and chairs. They stood by the double-hung windows that overlooked the street and afforded a perfect view of where both Nicholas Post and Scott Huntington had stood when the shooting happened.

Diego squirmed in the satchel, letting out a soft mew.

"Do you mind closing the door," Rosa said to Miguel. "I'm going to let Diego roam for a bit."

Rosa could tell that Miguel barely kept from rolling his eyes as she set the satchel on the floor and set her kitten free. He wasn't the type to run off and hide, but he did appreciate the freedom to sniff and climb. He jumped onto one of the tables and stared out the window.

Rosa fished out a magnifying glass from her purse.

"Nice," Miguel remarked. "Like Sherlock Holmes."

"Yes, well, where is yours?" she asked him.

"Good point."

Miguel glanced about the room. "I'm pretty sure it's Salvatore who was up here."

"You're probably right," Rosa said. She didn't blame Miguel for wanting to close this case quickly. His superintendent was clamoring for a quick arrest, and then there was that open wound created by Charlene Winters.

Rosa opened the first window and carefully examined the sill. Nothing.

Inexplicably, Diego hopped down from his perch on the table, approached the second windowsill, and sniffed.

"What have you found, Diego?" Rosa asked as she approached the second sill. There she saw a little residue and sniffed lightly. Familiar with the smell and look of gunshot residue, Rosa glanced at Miguel and back at the clue. Composed of tiny particles of primer and gunpowder, the residue had been expelled when a gun was fired. A faintly acrid smell of sulfur and urine made her want to gag. Instead, she ran a finger through the substance, then held it up in the air. "Smell this."

Miguel walked over and took a sniff.

"Aha," he said. "Someone definitely fired a shot from this window."

20

Miguel went back to the police headquarters, but Rosa decided to check in with her client. It was still premature to celebrate—after all, she didn't recommend that until after the killer was caught and arrested—but she did want to let Mr. Post know that he was likely off the hook and that her involvement on his behalf could end. She hung the straps of her satchel over her shoulder, and put a hand underneath the bottom to support her growing kitty.

"Let's go and see Mr. Post, Diego."

The walk over would give her time to mull things over, and her thoughts went to Charlene and Miguel's disconcerting behavior.

The movie set was in the process of being torn down. Until the production company could deal appropriately with public relations, the filming had been put on hold. A new actor would need to be hired, and Rosa had heard through Gloria that few actors wanted a role where the previous actor had been murdered, at least not until the murderer was apprehended.

The trailers remained at Miguel's request, at least for another day. If they didn't break the case soon, he'd have no legal recourse left to hold the prime suspects and if that happened, their leads had a very good chance of drying up and the case would likely grow cold.

The door to Mr. Post's trailer was closed, a sign he wasn't inside as it was too warm to not have it hanging open for extra air if one was inside. Rosa knocked on the door anyway.

"Mr. Post? It's Miss Reed. Are you in there?"

Rosa knocked again and even tried the door, but it was locked and Mr. Post was most certainly gone.

Diego chose this moment to wiggle about in the satchel and Rosa had to lay it on the grassy ground in order to give her arm a rest. "You're getting so big!"

Diego took the opportunity to hop out of the satchel, and even though he wore a collar, the leash wasn't attached. Rosa went to reach for him, but every time she got close, he hopped just out of reach.

"Silly bean. Come here!"

Rosa took a step, and Diego scampered away into the shade under Miss Williamson's trailer.

"Fine, be that way," Rosa said. She might as well wait a while to see if Mr. Post returned anyway.

Her gaze landed on Miss Williamson's trailer door, which was ajar. Every time the wind picked up, the door would open an inch then knock shut against the frame, though without enough energy to click shut.

"Miss Williamson?" Rosa called. She'd just assumed that the secretary was out with Mr. Post, but perhaps she was inside. The afternoon heat often drew people to their beds for short naps.

"Miss Williamson?" Since the door of the trailer was open, Rosa decided to step inside. It suddenly felt ominously quiet in the trailer area, and Rosa had a fleeting thought that Miss Williamson might be in trouble. It could be that Rosa wasn't the only woman in Mr. Post's sphere to encounter John Salvatore's bad side.

Ensuring Miss Williamson's well-being was enough incentive to enter the trailer without feeling like she was trespassing. A quick search confirmed that Miss Williamson was indeed out, and had failed to properly secure her door. As Rosa slipped inside the trailer, Diego ran in from behind, knocking her off balance onto the booth seat at the table.

"Diego!"

Rosa's disapproval of her feline was forgotten when her eyes settled on a notebook on the table, its pages splayed apart. A fragment of one of the pages was still attached to the coil-binding where the page had been torn off. A partial word remained: *Remin*. Probably the word *reminder*. A very common word to appear in a notepad.

The outline of the rest of the message was lightly engrained on the following blank page.

She stared at it for a moment, shook her head, and dropped her hands to her lap. She remembered how she had ridiculed the very thing she was about to do when she'd watched *The Last Clue*.

"And I told Larry that no detective had ever actually done this," she muttered to Diego, now curled up on the seat beside her. "So cliché!" Sighing, Rosa stared at the notepad for a moment longer, fished a pencil out of her purse, lightly rubbed it across the blank page then stared at the result. At the top of the page was the missing part of the word: *gton*.

Remington.

Just below that word in a smaller scribble was .357 *Magnum.*

Rosa knew there were several revolvers chambered for .357 Magnum rounds. She also knew that although a .357 Magnum round was slightly smaller than a .45, it could leave a similar path through a human body when fired at a relatively close range.

She wondered how much Mary Williamson knew about guns.

While Diego watched with narrow-eyed reproof, Rosa peeked inside two small cabinets, finding nothing of interest. Moving to the front of the trailer, she found a framed picture of Mary, her hair long and wavy, beside an older man next to the body of a black bear. The picture was shot in a forest clearing somewhere. The man was smiling, looking very proud, with one arm around Mary's shoulders. She, with a broad smile, held a rifle fitted with a scope in her right hand, the barrel lying across her left forearm. It was inscribed, *Daddy's little hunter.*

A chill shot through Rosa and without hesitation, she started a rapid search. Careful not to disrupt items, she opened every cupboard and drawer. She searched under the cushions, and in every possible crevice, but came up empty.

On a whim, she whipped open the portable refrigerator. Cans of soda and an overripe mango shared the two small shelves. All that was left was the tiny freezer unit. It was barely big enough to hold two ice cube trays, which happened to lie empty in the sink.

Instead of the trays, she found a single item in the freezer. Wrapped in oilcloth, a *Remington* .357

Magnum revolver with a modified barrel that looked like it had been fitted to receive a noise suppressor.

Suddenly, the door swung open, and Mary Williamson stepped in. The two women stared at each other. The secretary's eyes grew round, her mouth hung open, and her face flushed as red as her hair. Rosa held the weapon, partially wrapped in oilcloth, with both hands.

"You used a suppressor," Rosa said.

Miss Williamson turned and ran.

"Stay here, Diego!"

Rosa tossed the gun back into the freezer and chased after the secretary. Mary Williamson, with her hand on her hat, ran like a confused deer across the field to a narrow street that led to the square. Rosa, having chosen excellently that morning when she'd put on her capris and flats, sprinted after her.

As she ran past the food tents, she saw stunned crew members in the coffee tent staring after the fleeing form of Mary Williamson. At the edge of the tent, a uniformed security guard leaned on the tent's door pole holding a cup of coffee. As if he were pondering an interesting scene in a movie, he watched with a quizzical look on his face

Rosa slowed long enough to yell, "Someone call the police!" She pointed at the security guard. "You! Follow me!"

The young man just stood there, slowly stirring his coffee with his mouth half-open. He stared at Rosa.

"C'mon, Wyatt Earp! Coffee break is over!"

Up ahead, she saw her quarry disappear behind a red-brick building. Rosa chased after her, but when she rounded the second building, she found the street empty. The door to an ice cream shop was swinging shut.

At the far end of the street, Nicholas Post headed toward her with a perplexed look on his face.

"Miss Reed!" he shouted, "What's going on? I just saw . . ."

Ignoring him, Rosa ran into the ice cream shop. A teenage girl wearing a green apron held an ice cream scoop in the air. A quick scan of the room told Rosa that Mary Williamson wasn't among the customers seated in booths or on stools along the bar.

"Did a lady with red hair pass through here?"

"Good golly, yes. Whipped out the back!"

The back exit opened into an alley. Mary Williamson, lifting her skirt for better running, continued east. Winded, Miss Williamson's strides were slow.

"Miss Williamson!" Rosa called out. "You can't outrun me." Rosa had completed physical training at police training school in Britain and had always shown athletic aptitude.

Miss Williamson was undaunted. She knocked over a metal garbage can—spilling its contents all over the alley—stumbled, and after regaining her footing, disappeared around another corner.

Unfortunately for Miss Williamson, the alley ended in a brick dead end. Rosa found Mary Williamson pacing back and forth frantically in front of it. She then turned to face Rosa—her cheeks flushed, her breathing hard, and her eyes wild.

Rosa put out hands with her palms facing the ground. "Just calm down." Rosa was half expecting her quarry to rush to get past. But just as it seemed like the secretary was gathering herself to do just that, the security guard finally caught Rosa up. After a few hard-fought breaths, he muttered, "What's going on here?"

A moment later, Nicholas Post jogged up to them. "Mary?"

Anguish spread across Miss Williamson's face. She leaned against the brick wall; her shoulders slumped in defeat as she slid down to the ground. With quivering lips, she stared up at him.

Her voice cracked. "I did it for you, Nicholas. I love you. You know I do."

21

Standing behind the one-way glass partition of an interrogation room at the Santa Bonita police station, Rosa watched Miguel and Detective Sanchez sit down at a table opposite Mary Williamson. The secretary's eyes were bloodshot and puffy, and her bony hands trembled as she sipped on a cup of tea that an officer had provided. She was the picture of someone with little resistance left; Rosa recognized the look. It was unmistakable. Mary Williamson was on the brink of a confession.

"I promise you, you will be treated fairly here," Miguel said.

Miss Williamson nodded and wiped one eye with her hand.

Sanchez placed a box of tissues within reach.

Miguel perused his notes. "We have gunpowder

residue from the windowsill above the restaurant where you took the shot, and we have the murder weapon belonging to you, and the bullet and casing that came from the shot. Forensics has confirmed that the angle of the bullet trajectory that killed Mr. Huntington came from that second-floor window and has proven that it didn't come from the prop gun used by Mr. Post." He glanced briefly at Sanchez, then addressed her, "Did you shoot Scott Huntington, Miss Williamson? It will go better for you if you cooperate."

Mary Williamson nodded while holding a tissue to her face. Her carefully brushed-on mascara ran down her cheeks.

"I need you to answer out loud for the tape machine," Miguel said in a soft voice.

"Yes, I shot him."

"The question we are all asking ourselves, Miss Williamson, is why?" Sanchez said.

"I love Nicholas." The tremor in her voice strengthened with determination. "What he and I have is special! My job, my *life* . . . is to make sure the world recognizes him for who he is—the greatest actor that ever walked onto the silver screen."

Using the tissue, she blew in a rather brash manner then continued with a tone of defiance. "The first time I saw him, I knew we were destined to be together and that my calling in life was to be close to him, to hold him up to the light."

"How long have you worked for Mr. Post?" Miguel asked.

"Seven years. I know it sounds like a long time, but I'm a very patient person, Detective Belmonte. It was only a matter of time, once Nicholas *really* got to know me, that he'd see what I see. We were meant to be together."

Miguel leaned in. "How does Scott Huntington fit into this?"

Rosa was eager to know the answer to this question too. From the way Miss Williamson was talking, Rosa was surprised that Charlene wasn't the one who'd been gunned down.

"Scott Huntington? Ha!" Miss Williamson laughed bitterly, her eyes wild, darting between Miguel and Detective Sanchez. "He was such a hack! Anybody with any brains could see that. But he was always stealing the spotlight . . . a spotlight that he did not deserve, *and* he flaunted it. All those magazine articles, comparing him to Nicholas, saying that he was the better actor. What a joke! What a travesty."

She teared up again. "Nicholas and I had many conversations about Scott. Late at night, when everyone else was gone, and the cameras stopped rolling, he had me—*only me*—to commiserate with, didn't he? He even started to doubt himself after the last article came out. Well . . ." She nodded her head vigorously. "That's when I started putting together this little plan. I knew that waitress would be out of the building during the shooting scene. After all, she's a *real* Nicholas Post fan. I reckoned she'd come outside to get a better look, and I was right."

"Was Mr. Post in on the planning?" Miguel asked. "The prop gun was used in rehearsal, and according to Mr. Dennis McCann, that was an unscheduled decision. But the fact is, it would have given you more opportunity to pull this off. I mean, you had to wait for just the right moment to shoot because of the sound, *and* you had to hit your target. It would have given you more than one chance to get it right if you knew Nicholas Post was going to use the gun during rehearsal."

"No," Miss Williamson shook her head. "He'd never agree to do something like this. The decision to use the gun at rehearsal was a surprise even to me, but in the end, it played into my plan nicely. Opened up more rabbit trails for you to follow." Her lips tugged up into a subtle smile. "As for getting it right, well, that was easy. I just had to watch when he pointed. From my position, I could see the hammer pull back on his revolver."

Rosa mused that Miss Williamson's statement

was true. Rosa felt confident that she could've made that shot. A person only had to be very familiar with the script and the timing, which Mr. Post's secretary was.

Miss Williamson let out a long, sad sigh. "I knew you wouldn't keep Nicholas as a suspect for very long. I mean, I love Nicholas with all my heart, but he couldn't hit the broadside of a red barn!"

She smiled through her tears as if remembering some pleasant memory. "I knew you would figure out that he couldn't have done it, but I still thought it best to hire a detective to make sure. Of course, I never dreamed Miss Reed would actually . . ." She let the sentence go unfinished and just shook her head. "Anyway, it worked out perfectly that Nicholas spent the break with that blonde hussy. What's her name? Charlotte or—"

Miguel tugged at his tie, his expression pinched. "Charlene Winters."

"Yes, that's it. I had a feeling he would do that; he'd been flirting with her a few times already." She shrugged her shoulders. "Anyway, Mr. McCann would be a much better suspect. I figured you might arrest him. He knows about guns, after all. He also had the most access to the revolver."

"Speaking of which," Miguel began, "it took some marksmanship to pull that shot off."

"Not to mention some knowledge about guns," Sanchez added.

"I grew up in Wisconsin, Detectives." Pride flashed behind her eyes. "Statewide Junior Champion three years in a row. I can shoot through a silver dollar at thirty paces. My dad has all my trophies sitting on the family fireplace. He taught me everything I know about guns and how to use them." She smiled weakly. "I had that revolver fitted for a silencer in Los Angeles at a gun shop in Compton. I knew that it was an odd request, but that Remington is the gun I learned to shoot with." Then her smile disappeared. "When I saw that Miss Reed had found it and that she recognized it had been fitted for a suppressor . . . I knew it was over. Why else would she search my trailer? Why else would I have had that gun modified?

"But I have a question?" Mary Williamson said. "How did Miss Reed know to check *my* trailer. I mean, sure you found gunpowder but . . ." Her eyes suddenly widened. "It was Mr. Salvatore, wasn't it?"

"What do you mean?" Miguel asked

"He said it was our secret and that he wouldn't tell. He even thanked me. Oh, that scoundrel!"

"Miss Williamson, I am afraid I don't follow. Did he have a part in your plan?"

"No!" Her eyes rolled backwards and she shook her head like the truth was obvious. "He saw me! After

I took the shot, I turned to leave, and Mr. Salvatore was standing at the top of the stairs with a gun in his hand and a big smile on his face."

Miguel turned to the one-way mirror, staring at Rosa as if he could see her. If he thought she knew something about this, he was wrong.

22

Rosa didn't know if she liked having her name in the paper, but she had to admit it brought certain perks. An article had come out in the *Santa Bonita Post* two weeks ago about a murder investigation that involved two famous movie stars at a film shoot in the Spanish quarter. It had mentioned that "Santa Bonita's own" Rosa Reed had been hired by Mr. Post. The fact that she'd worked in cooperation with the Santa Bonita Police Department was a marketing coup, leading to her phone at Reed Investigations ringing nonstop.

Mary Williamson was under psychiatric assessment. Rosa was thankful, for Miss Williamson's sake, that the practice of performing frontal lobotomies on the insane to cure such ills was going out of favor.

There was a warrant out for the arrest of John

Salvatore, also known on the east coast as Johnny Shooter. Miguel could not track him down and put out a nationwide APB. The newshounds reported that Mr. Salvatore had been hired by the Patriarchi family to assassinate Scott Huntington in retaliation for putting one of the Patriarchi daughters in the family way and refusing to marry her.

Only, in a strange twist of fate, Mary Williamson had done the deed before he could.

Gloria, still floundering with self-direction, had taken Rosa's offer to help with work in her office—answering the phone and filing paperwork. While studying her long painted fingernails, she said, "I'm thinking about studying journalism."

Rosa looked up from the photographs from her most recent case that she was studying: a runaway she'd found hiding out in a commune in the hills. She'd sent copies of the prints to the girl's worried parents in LA, proving their daughter was alive and where she could be located.

"Again?" Rosa said. Gloria had brought journalism up as a possibility for her life's purpose before.

"I'm serious this time," Gloria said defensively. "Working for you has opened my eyes to the complexities of the human psyche. I've been living in a bubble for much too long."

Rosa couldn't argue with that. And Gloria was far

too intelligent to simply do nothing. "It's a good idea if you're serious. Just make sure you are. Jumping from thing to thing does nothing for your credibility. Perhaps you should give it some time to percolate before acting upon it."

Gloria jutted her chin in the air. "I can work for you while I wait. You don't have to pay me; I'll be an intern. You'll see that I mean what I'm saying this time."

The telephone rang, and Diego, from his favorite spot on the sofa, opened his eyes briefly before falling back to sleep.

Gloria sang into the receiver, "Reed Investigations . . . Oh, hello!"

Rosa shot Gloria a look. Gloria recognized the caller—and Miguel's face came to mind. Rosa had asked him to let her know if he heard anything about Miss Williamson's trial and verdict. Nicholas Post was already lined up for a new film, again directed by Fredrick Forbes. Most of the crew of *Quick Strike* was also involved, including Mr. McCann and Miss Vickers. Charlene Winters was the only name not listed among them.

On a personal level, Rosa wanted to know how Miguel was holding up after Charlene's betrayal. As Clarence had pointed out, Santa Bonita wasn't a big place, and news of one of their detectives breaking off his engagement, and the speculative reasons, was the talk of the town.

She stared at Gloria, her eyebrow shooting up in question.

Gloria stepped away from her desk as she held out the receiver. "It's Dr. Rayburn."

For a split second, Rosa felt a twinge of disappointment, but quickly recovered, and answered with sincere joy in her voice. "Larry! Is this business or pleasure?"

"Thankfully, pleasure! Guess who's coming to Santa Bonita?"

"I really couldn't."

"Elvis Presley!"

Rosa couldn't hold in her surprise. *"Really?"* After the popstar's performance on *The Ed Sullivan Show*—which the whole Forrester clan had gathered around their television to watch, Larry included—Rosa had imagined the man's fame had soared.

"He was booked to play at the Veterans' Theater before he aired on *Sullivan*, and he's keepin' to his tour schedule. He'll be here next month, and I got tickets! I know you like music and dancin'. You'll come with me, won't you?"

Rosa needed a good diversion from the low-grade turmoil brewing gently beneath the surface. It looked like Miguel would be single again—Charlene had left town with the other actors—but it didn't mean Rosa and Miguel could rekindle what they once had. That was a *fairy tale* Rosa needed to stomp out at once. Miguel was in mourning over what had happened with *Charlene*, and probably not thinking about Rosa at all.

Determined to ignore her puzzling feelings and enjoy her life, she focused on the voice on the other end of the line.

"Yes, Larry, I'd love that. I wouldn't miss it for the world!

∽

If you enjoyed reading *Murder on Location* please help others enjoy it too.

Recommend it: Help others find the book by recommending it to friends, readers' groups, discussion boards and by **suggesting it to your local library.**

Review it: Please tell other readers why you liked this book by reviewing it on Amazon or Goodreads.

EAGER TO READ the next book in the Rosa Reed Mystery series?

Don't miss *Murder and Rock 'n Roll,* A Rosa Reed Mystery # 5.

Murder is a hit!

It's the summer of 1956 and Private Investigator Rosa Reed (former Woman Police Constable from the London Metropolitan Police) attends her first rock and roll concert featuring the young and upcoming music sensation Elvis Presley. The high note goes sour when a press photographer is found dead onstage and Rosa is called in to investigate. When the apparent suicide is deemed to be a murder, she is once again called upon to work side by side with her former flame, Detective Miguel Belmonte. Will Rosa keep her heart in line and find the killer before she has to sing the blues?

Find it on Amazon

Read on for a Sneak Peak!

Did you read the PREQUEL?

Rosa & Miguel's Wartime Romance is a BONUS short story exclusively for Lee's newsletter subscribers.

How it All Began...

Like many British children during World War Two, Rosa Reed's parents, Ginger and Basil Reed, made the heart-wrenching decision to send their child to a foreign land and out of harm's way. Fortunately, Ginger's half-sister Louisa and her family, now settled in the quaint coastal town of Santa Bonita, California, were pleased to take her in.

By the spring of 1945, Rosa Reed had almost made it through American High School unscathed, until the American army decided to station a base there. Until she met the handsome Private Miguel Belmonte and fell in love...

READ FREE!

Start from the beginning ~ Murder on the SS Rosa!

Find it on Amazon

Also on AUDIO!

Read on for an excerpt.

ROSA & MIGUEL'S WARTIME ROMANCE
PREQUEL - EXCERPT

Rosa Reed first laid eyes on Miguel Belmonte on the fourteenth day of February in 1945. She was a senior attending a high school dance, and he a soldier who played in the band.

She'd been dancing with her date, Tom Hawkins, a short, stalky boy with pink skin and an outbreak of acne, but her gaze continued to latch onto the bronze-skinned singer, with dark crew-cut hair, looking very dapper in a black suit.

In a life-changing moment, their eyes locked. Despite the fact that she stared at the singer over the shoulder of her date, she couldn't help the bolt of electricity that shot through her, and when the singer smiled—and those dimples appeared—heavens, her knees almost gave out!

"Rosa?"

Tom's worried voice brought her back to reality. "Are you okay? You went a little limp there. Do you feel faint? It is mighty hot in here." Tom released Rosa's hand to tug at his tie. "Do you want to get some air?"

Rosa felt a surge of alarm. Invitations to step outside the gymnasium were often euphemisms to get fresh.

In desperation she searched for her best friend Nancy Davidson—her best *American* friend, that was. Vivien Eveleigh claimed the position of *best* friend back in London, and Rosa missed her. Nancy made for a sufficient substitute. A pretty girl with honey-blond hair, Nancy, fortunately, was no longer dancing, and was sitting alone.

"I think I'll visit the ladies, Tom, if you don't mind."

He looked momentarily put out, then shrugged. "Suit yourself." He joined a group of lads—boys—at the punch table, and joined in with their raucous laughter. Rosa didn't want to know what they were joking about, or at whose expense.

Nancy understood Rosa's plight as she wasn't entirely pleased with her fellow either. "If only you and I could dance with each other."

"One can't very well go to a dance without a date, though," Rosa said.

Nancy laughed. "*One* can't."

Rosa rolled her eyes. Even after four years of living in America, her Englishness still manifested when she was distracted.

And tonight's distraction was the attractive lead singer in the band, and shockingly, he seemed to have sought her face out too.

Nancy had seen the exchange and gave Rosa a firm nudge. "No way, José. I know he's cute, but he's from the wrong side of the tracks. Your aunt would have a conniption."

Nancy wasn't wrong about that. Aunt Louisa had very high standards, as one who was lady of Forrester mansion, might.

"I'm only looking!"

Nancy harrumphed. "As long as it stays that way."

Continue reading >>>

Rosa & Miguel's Wartime Romance is a BONUS short story exclusively for Lee's newsletter subscribers.

Subscribe Now!

SNEAK PEEK ~ MURDER AND ROCK 'N ROLL
CHAPTER ONE

*D*espite her efforts to restrain bubbling excitement, to enlist the calm instilled by her British upbringing with its emphasis on keeping a "stiff upper lip", Rosa Reed couldn't help but let out a low-pitched squeal. This uncharacteristic sound escaping her lips, newly coated in a tangerine lipstick, aroused her sleepy cat Diego, who curled up in the center of her four-poster bed. He glared at her through narrow, smoky-green eyes.

Rosa emitted a chuckle and rubbed his ears vigorously in retaliation. "I know it means nothing to you, Diego, but it's *Elvis Presley!*"

A year previous, Rosa would've been hard pressed to recite a tidbit of trivia about the young music star, but now it was like Elvis Presley was everywhere—one couldn't' get away from hearing his music on the radio, seeing his face on the cover of magazines and watching him on Ed Sullivan. And he was in Santa Bonita!

Pure serendipity, since the concert had been booked before Elvis had become a national sensation. Rosa's main squeeze, Dr. Larry Rayburn, who was the town's assistant medical examiner, had gotten tickets and Rosa couldn't wait for their date to begin. She turned back to her bedroom mirror and added finishing touches to her makeup. After agonizing over several outfits, Rosa had decided on a two-tone navy blue and red dress with a form-fitting bodice that accentuated her new "bullet bra", and a flouncy red skirt with a full crinoline slip which she thought would be fun for an upbeat concert such as an Elvis Presley concert promised to be. She suspected that many of the concert attendees would be teenagers, and though she was closer to thirty than twenty, Rosa felt young at heart, perhaps because, despite a failed attempt, she'd yet to marry and start a family.

The melody of *Blue Moon*, a song that had been playing a lot on local radio, reached Rosa from down the hall. Rosa, recently relocated to California from London, England, lived with her American relatives in a very large estate known as the Forrester mansion. Gloria Forrester, Rosa's cousin who *was* closer to twenty than thirty, was preparing to go to the concert as well, along with her friend Marjorie.

"Without a dream in my haaaaert" they sang loudly in unison. Rosa had to see what the two girls were up to, and tapped on the partially opened door before entering Gloria's colorful bedroom.

"Oh, Rosa," Gloria trilled. "I'm so excited, my knees are like marshmallows!"

Marjorie stared at the cardboard cover of the long playing record they were listing to and swooned over the picture of Elvis, his smiling face large and inviting. "He's just so dreamy!"

Rosa laughed. "I hope you two will survive the night." She looked to Marjorie. "Is your sister going to be there?"

Nancy Kline was a friend of Rosa's from their high school years, when Rosa had lived with the Forrester family to escape the dangers of German bombs over London. Her own parents, Basil and Ginger Reed had stayed behind, and Rosa suspected they'd done covert work for the government, but both were frustratingly vague about those years.

"Yes," Marjorie said. "She practically had to force Eddie to take her. I told her she could go with us, but I guess we're too uncivilized for her. I swear, sometimes she acts older than our mother."

"Three young sons might do that to a person," Rosa said.

Gloria and Marjorie acted like teenagers, but they

were in their early twenties and most girls their age were either married or engaged. But Rosa could hardly preach. She missed out on marrying her high-school sweetheart, Miguel Belmonte, who now happened to be a detective in the Santa Bonita police force. Their romance had been short but severe, forbidden by Aunt Louisa and forced to an end when World War Two was over and Rosa had been sent back to England.

Now she had Larry, a funny and kind Texan on her arm, and Rosa couldn't be more thankful.

Yes, she was thankful.

Even though Miguel's engagement to Charlene Winters had dissolved, rather, had disintegrated, and in a shockingly public way.

Miguel was single again, but she was not, and she wouldn't break the heart of a sincere and lovely man, because she was in love once before as a teenager.

It wouldn't be fair.

Returning to her bedroom, Rosa scooped Diego off the bed, then headed down the staircase, along the wide hallway, and to the kitchen at the back of the mansion. Señora Gomez, the long-time housekeeper, greeted Rosa and Diego with her standard warm smile.

"You look really nice, Miss Rosa."

"Thank you. I hope I'm not overdressed."

"This Elvis fellow is very famous now, eh?"

"They call him an overnight sensation."

Rosa set Diego on the tile floor and he immediately investigated the status of his food and water bowls, both full, thanks to Señora Gomez.

Through the vast windows Rosa spotted two members of her American family, and joined them on the patio overlooking the pool, tennis court and vast gardens. Palm trees dotted the well-manicured lawns and Rosa loved the tropical essence the trees evoked. The mansion itself was a sprawling mission-style edifice that had Rosa gasping in admiration, even on her second visit.

"Join us for a cocktail?" The invitation came from Aunt Louisa, technically Rosa's half aunt as she and Rosa's mother, Ginger, shared a father but not a mother. Dressed in a top of the line blue satin cocktail dress with triangular capped sleeves, and a waist narrow enough to make a much younger woman envious, her aunt gave off the sophistication that her wealth and status demanded. Rosa hardly felt she could refuse. She lowered herself on the edge of one of the loungers, not wanting to get too comfortable, as she expected Larry to arrive soon.

"Just a small one," Rosa said. "I'll be leaving shortly."

Aunt Louisa called to Ricardo, the pool boy, who hovered nearby. "A piña colada for Miss Reed." She glanced at Rosa for approval, and Rosa nodded her head.

"Are you going to that Elvis Presley thing?" Sally Hartigan asked, a hint of her Boston accent remaining. The eldest occupant of the Forrester mansion was Aunt Louisa's Boston born mother and though not related to Rosa by blood, she insisted Rosa call her Grandma Sally. The lady's permanently tanned face had wrinkled through her seventy-plus years, but her grey hair was professionally permed and her dress tailored just for her, and perfectly pressed. She lifted a glass of amber that tinkled with ice in Rosa's direction.

"Yes," Rosa answered. "I'm waiting for Larry to pick me up."

Grandma Sally scowled. "I've seen Mr. Presley on television. The way he wiggles about onstage is uncouth."

"It's the new music, mother," Aunt Louisa said, taking a sip of her drink. "Rock and Roll."

"It's vulgar," Grandma Sally muttered. "Young people these days have no manners. No respect for their elders."

"I'm sure they're not all like that," Rosa said. Ricardo returned with the piña colada, attractively garnished with a slice of fresh pineapple, and Rosa thanked him before taking a sip.

Grandma Sally was insistent. "It's not safe to cross

the street. Just the other day we were nearly run over by a young man speeding down main, his radio blaring and wearing glasses so dark, no wonder he couldn't see. Didn't we, Louisa?"

"I'm going to talk to the mayor about putting in another set of traffic lights," Aunt Louisa said. "And a lower speed limit. Something they'll enforce. What do the police do around Santa Bonita, anyway?"

Rosa and her aunt didn't land on the same side when it came to their opinions about the police. Rosa's job as a private investigator often caused her path to cross with the local men in blue, along with a certain well-dressed detective that her aunt had never forgiven. Rosa found it best to steer away from the topic when it came up.

"And don't forget," Aunt Louisa continued, "our annual fundraiser for the Santa Bonita Veteran's Foundation is happening in a few days at the very same theater you're going to tonight." She raised a dark, professionally plucked eyebrow at Rosa. "I hope you marked it on your calendar."

"Oh yes. I am looking forward to that," Rosa returned, thankful that they'd moved off the subject of the police.

Señora Gomez entered the patio with quick steps. "Telephone for you, Miss Rosa," she called out. "It's your doctor amigo."

Rosa checked her watch. Larry should be driving his truck up their drive by now, not calling on the telephone. She excused herself and followed Señora Gomez back into the kitchen where she picked up the receiver.

"Larry?"

"Hello, darlin'," Larry said.

Rosa thought his voice sounded a little weak. "Are you all right?"

"I'm as sick as a dog, darlin'. I'm sorry to do this to ya, but I can't make it to the concert tonight."

"Oh, no." Rosa's heart dropped. As much as she was concerned for Larry's health, she was dreadfully disappointed not to go to the Elvis Presley concert.

As if he read her mind, he said, "You can still go. I'll send a cabbie to you with the tickets. Maybe you could take a friend."

Rosa's mind worked hurriedly. She could go with Gloria and Marjorie, and perhaps she could convince Clarence to join them. Since his wife had left him and his young daughter, he did nothing but mope about. It would be good for him.

"If you don't mind?"

"Not at all. I'd feel terrible if you missed out on my account. You're doin' me a favor by goin'."

"Well, if you're certain."

His warm Texan accent reassured her. "Darn tootin', I am."

It was a consolation prize, but Rosa took it."

"Thank you, Larry. I'll take pictures and be sure to tell you all about it. It's going to be a momentous event."

Find it on Amazon

EXCERPT ~ MURDER ON THE SS ROSA

CHAPTER 1

In the dismal autumn of 1918 Ginger Gold had vowed she'd never go back to Europe. Yet here she was, five years later in 1923, aboard the SS *Rosa* as it traversed the Atlantic from Boston to Liverpool.

"Isn't a dinner invitation from the captain reserved for *very important persons?*" Haley Higgins asked.

Ginger propped a hand on her tiny waist and feigned insult. "Are you suggesting that I'm not a very important person?"

"I'd never suggest such a thing," Haley said lightly. "Only that I'm not aware of your connection to him."

"Oh, yes. Father used to travel to England once or twice a year for business, and they had made an acquaintance. Of course, this was some years ago, before Father fell ill. Captain Walsh recognised my name on the passenger list. It was nice of him to extend an invitation, was it not?"

Haley nodded. "I expect it to be quite entertaining."

Ginger chose a billowy, violet dropped-waist frock with a hem that ended near her ankles, nude stockings with seams that ran up the back of her slender legs, and black designer T-strap heels. She clipped on dangling earrings and patted the ends of her bobbed red hair with the palms of her gloved hands. She made a show of presenting herself.

"How do I look?"

"Gorgeous, as always," Haley said. Long since dressed, she waited patiently in a rose-coloured upholstered chair. She was the sensible type, having only packed a few tweed and linen suits. She wasn't much for "presentation." It made getting ready quick and painless.

Curled up on the silky pink quilted cover on Ginger's bed was a small, short-haired black and white dog. Ginger scrubbed him behind his pointed ears and kissed his forehead. "You're such a good boy, Boss." The Boston terrier's stub of a tail wagged in agreement.

Ginger finished her ensemble by draping a creamy silk shawl over her shoulders. "Shall we?" Ginger said, motioning to the door.

Boss stood and stretched his hind legs.

"Oh, sorry, Bossy. Not you this time."

The dog let out a snort of disappointment, then circled his pillow before settling and swiftly fell back to sleep.

"I love the sea! Don't you?" Ginger said as she and Haley walked along an exterior corridor of the ship. She extended her youthful arms and inhaled exuberantly. "It's one of the reasons I love Boston. So invigorating. Makes one feel alive!"

"Oh, honey, listen to you!" Haley said with amusement. "Your latent Britishness is becoming more pronounced the closer we get to England."

"Makes *one* feel alive," she added, mimicking Ginger's sudden use of an English accent.

Though Ginger considered herself a Bostonian through and through, she embraced her English heritage. After all, Massachusetts *was* part of New *England.*

"You're jolly well right, old thing," Ginger admitted with an exaggerated English accent. She laughed heartily, bringing a smile to Haley's normally stoic expression.

"You sounded like your father just now," Haley said.

Ginger placed a hand on her heart. "Oh, I do miss him."

"Me, too."

"In his honour I shall be thoroughly British for the duration of my time abroad."

A smile spread across Haley's wide face. "And you'll do it charmingly."

Ginger threaded her arm through her friend's. "Soon-to-be Doctor Higgins," she said. "We mustn't keep the captain waiting."

"If you insist, Mrs. Gold," Haley returned, then added, "You know, I think the captain has eyes for you."

"*Pfft.* How can you say that? We only met him for a second." Ginger flicked her gloved hand. "Besides, he's got a wife."

"With men like the captain," Haley said stiffly, "I hardly think that matters."

***

A wide, modern staircase with lush red carpeting led to an elegant first-class dining room on the top deck.

"Posh," Haley said. "I'm not sure I fit in here."

"Nonsense," Ginger responded airily. "You're with me!"

Haley scoffed lightly. "An accessory? I'm certainly not flamboyant enough to suit your style."

Ginger laughed, a spritely laugh her husband, Daniel, once had said reminded him of fairies dancing in a waterfall.

"You are on the inside, my dear Haley. That's what counts."

The red carpet continued throughout the restaurant, accenting jade-green and dusty rose upholstered chairs placed in groups of four around round, brass-trimmed chestnut tables.

"There they are," Ginger said, and led the way to where their hosts were seated.

Captain Walsh was an attractive man of average height and weight. His thick dark hair was greying slightly at the temples. He stood when he identified them, exuding authority. "Mrs. Gold. It's a pleasure."

"The pleasure is ours," Ginger said, shaking the captain's hand. His palm was large but soft, and he wore a wide ring that brandished a flat section of jade. The sleeve of his shirt slipped past the four stripes on the cuff of his jacket, and Ginger noted a handsome cuff link, a shiny silver piece embossed with a fleur-de-lis.

Motioning to Haley, she added, "This is my companion, Miss Higgins."

The captain's smile remained as he offered his hand. "Good to meet you."

Haley shook his hand with vice-grip confidence. "Likewise."

"May I introduce my wife, Mrs. Walsh." The thin woman on his right wore a dated late-Edwardian smock that was cinched at the waist. Her overly upright posture indicated that she most certainly wore an antiquated corset. She nodded in greeting, but refrained from offering a hand or even a smile. Ginger blamed the corset for her poor temperament.

"Nice to meet you, Mrs. Walsh." Ginger took the seat next to the captain while Haley positioned herself beside his wife.

"Please let me express my appreciation at your kind invitation to join you on our first night," Ginger said. "I'm sure these seats are much coveted!"

"It is my delight to have the daughter of Mr. Hartigan onboard. Your father was a respectable gentleman, and I'm honoured to have known him. I only wish he were alive and with us here today."

"As do I." Ginger patted Haley's arm. "Miss Higgins, his personal nurse through his last years, showed him the compassion and respect he deserved. She was also a tremendous comfort to my little sister and stepmother. I really don't know what we would've done without her." Ginger's praise of Haley was sincere, but she also hoped a good character reference would erase any prejudice forthcoming due to her friend's unorthodox attire.

"How fortunate that she could accompany you to London," Mrs. Walsh said with a crisp English accent.

"Indeed, it is stupendously good fortune," Ginger said. "Just as I was making plans to attend to my father's London estate, Miss Higgins learned she would continue her medical training there."

Mrs. Walsh looked astounded. "A lady doctor?"

"Many doors are opening for the modern woman, Mrs. Walsh," Haley responded. "In fact, the institution in question is the London School of Medicine for Women."

"But why London?" Captain Walsh asked. "Though I'm the first to acknowledge how fine the city is, surely there is a prestigious facility in America?"

"Yes, of course," Haley said. "I completed two years at Boston University before enlisting in the war." A shadow flickered behind her eyes. "You could say I was ready for a change of scenery." The catalyst for change was Haley's fiancé, who, despite potential social repercussions, had unceremoniously broken off their relationship to pursue another woman.

Before the captain or Mrs. Walsh could probe further, Ginger interjected, "Miss Higgins served as a nurse during the war, both in France and England. She developed an affection for London, didn't you, *old girl?*"

Ginger laughed at her use of the English parlance, and Haley smirked. "I did, indeed."

A waiter took their drink orders, and when he returned, Ginger accepted her glass of fine French wine with relish. "Even though we're no longer in the States, I can't help but feel guilty." She cast a slight glance over her shoulder and laughed. "I half-expect a federal Prohibition agent to arrest me any minute!"

"You are quite safe," Captain Walsh said with a smile. "This vessel is under the command of His Royal Highness, who, on occasion, happens to enjoy a drink or two."

Ginger sipped daintily as she allowed the fruity sensation to tingle her mouth before swallowing. She sighed with contentment.

Mrs. Walsh attempted to pick up her glass, but the captain moved it out of reach. "Not for you. You know what occurs when you drink too much." Mrs. Walsh's lips pursed in anger, but she stayed silent.

Ginger and Haley shared a look. If the captain was watching out for his wife, he certainly wasn't subtle. The heat of Mrs. Walsh's embarrassment stretched across the table.

Thankfully, the meal arrived, dissipating the situation. Ginger's mouth watered at the sight of roasted lamb with mint sauce, roast potatoes, and buttered green beans. The smell was heavenly. The chief cook, a rotund man with a ruddy complexion and dark eyes, hovered beside the captain, waiting for his assessment.

Captain Walsh made a point of chewing well, and followed the morsel up with a sip of chardonnay. "It's good, Babineaux."

After her first bite, Ginger added enthusiastically, "Simply delicious!"

Babineaux ducked his chin, then cast a glance at Mrs. Walsh. A look passed between them as the woman nodded her approval, allowing for a smile. Had Ginger imagined it, or had something more meaningful than a culinary rating been communicated?

A beautiful woman sat at a table across the room. Ginger recognised her as Nancy Guilford, the famous American actress. In her company were several gentlemen—one Ginger thought to be particularly dapper—and a middle-aged female companion. Ginger admired Miss Guilford's exotic, long-waisted ocean-blue oriental gown trimmed in fur. Her wavy blonde bob exposed diamond earrings that glistened in the electric light, and her lips were thick and bright red.

"Patty, darlin'," Nancy Guilford said with a loud New Jersey accent. Her voice was surprisingly nasal. Not at all what a person would expect from such a beautiful and sophisticated face. "Hand me my ciggies."

Her companion delivered a package of cigarettes, which Miss Guilford opened with graceful fingers. She placed a cigarette into an ivory-coloured holder and held it to her lips. One of the men (not the dapper one, Ginger was happy to note) rapidly produced a brass lighter and offered a flame. Miss Guilford inhaled, then let out a long stream of smoke in the captain's direction.

Though it was a simple, routine, everyday activity —a mere inhale and exhale—Nancy Guilford had made a compelling performance out of it. Even if someone present hadn't recognised the actress, her flair and charisma commanded attention. Ginger was sure the entire room had noticed her. Mrs. Walsh in particular seemed agitated. She glared at Miss Guilford with jealousy and suspicion in her eyes.

Ginger didn't think Mrs. Walsh was being paranoid in the least. The blonde stared shamelessly at the captain, going out of her way to present a creamy, *bare* calf when she crossed her legs.

Oh, mercy.

Captain Walsh pulled at his collar and pretended not to notice. The four of them returned to polite conversation, interspersed with comments on the quality of the food and the splendour of the dining room.

Throughout the meal, the captain, when his eyes weren't straying to the glamorous actress, watched Ginger in a way that left her feeling slightly uncomfortable. She feared Haley's assessment of him was all too correct.

Find it on AMAZON
Also on audio!

MORE FROM LEE STRAUSS

On AMAZON

THE ROSA REED MYSTERIES

(1950s cozy historical)

Murder at High Tide

Murder on the Boardwalk

Murder at the Bomb Shelter

Murder on Location

Murder and Rock 'n Roll

Murder at the Races

Murder at the Dude Ranch

Murder in London

Murder at the Fiesta

Murder at the Weddings

GINGER GOLD MYSTERY SERIES (cozy 1920s historical)

Cozy. Charming. Filled with Bright Young Things. This Jazz Age murder mystery will entertain and delight you with its 1920s flair and pizzazz!

Murder on the SS Rosa

Murder at Hartigan House

Murder at Bray Manor

Murder at Feathers & Flair

Murder at the Mortuary

Murder at Kensington Gardens

Murder at St. George's Church

The Wedding of Ginger & Basil

Murder Aboard the Flying Scotsman

Murder at the Boat Club

Murder on Eaton Square

Murder by Plum Pudding

Murder on Fleet Street

Murder at Brighton Beach

Murder in Hyde Park

Murder at the Royal Albert Hall

Murder in Belgravia

Murder on Mallowan Court

Murder at the Savoy

Murder at the Circus

Murder in France

Murder at Yuletide

LADY GOLD INVESTIGATES (Ginger Gold companion short stories)

Volume 1

Volume 2

Volume 3

Volume 4

HIGGINS & HAWKE MYSTERY SERIES (cozy 1930s historical)

The 1930s meets Rizzoli & Isles in this friendship depression era cozy mystery series.

Death at the Tavern

Death on the Tower

Death on Hanover

Death by Dancing

A NURSERY RHYME MYSTERY SERIES (mystery/sci fi)

Marlow finds himself teamed up with intelligent and savvy Sage Farrell, a girl so far out of his league he feels blinded in her presence - literally - damned glasses! Together they work to find the identity of @gingerbreadman. Can they stop the killer before he strikes again?

Gingerbread Man

Life Is but a Dream

Hickory Dickory Dock

Twinkle Little Star

LIGHT & LOVE (sweet romance)

Set in the dazzling charm of Europe, follow Katja, Gabriella, Eva, Anna and Belle as they find strength, hope and love.

Love Song

Your Love is Sweet

In Light of Us

Lying in Starlight

PLAYING WITH MATCHES (WW2 history/romance)

A sobering but hopeful journey about how one young German boy copes with the war and propaganda. Based on true events.

A Piece of Blue String (companion short story)

THE CLOCKWISE COLLECTION (YA time travel romance)

Casey Donovan has issues: hair, height and uncontrollable trips to the 19th century! And now this ~ she's accidentally taken Nate Mackenzie, the cutest boy in the school, back in time. Awkward.

Clockwise

Clockwiser

Like Clockwork

Counter Clockwise

Clockwork Crazy

Clocked (companion novella)

Standalones

Seaweed

Love, Tink

ABOUT THE AUTHORS

Lee Strauss is a USA TODAY bestselling author of The Ginger Gold Mysteries series, The Higgins & Hawke Mystery series, The Rosa Reed Mystery series (cozy historical mysteries), A Nursery Rhyme Mystery series (mystery suspense), The Perception series (young adult dystopian), The Light & Love series (sweet romance), The Clockwise Collection (YA time travel romance), and young adult historical fiction with over a million books read. She has titles published in German, Spanish and Korean, and a growing audio library.

When Lee's not writing or reading she likes to cycle, hike, and watch the ocean. She loves to drink caffè lattes and red wines in exotic places, and eat dark chocolate anywhere.

Denise Jaden is the author of several contemporary novels for teens and nonfiction books for writers. She splits her time between writing, dancing with a Polynesian dance troupe, and acting with the Vancouver film industry. Find out more about Denise at denise-jaden.com.

Norm Strauss is a singer-songwriter and performing artist who's seen the stage of The Voice of Germany. Short story writing is a new passion he shares with his wife Lee Strauss. Check out Norm's music page www.normstrauss.com

For more info on books by Lee Strauss and her social media links, visit leestraussbooks.com. To make sure you don't miss the next new release, be sure to sign up for her readers' list!

Did you know you can follow your favorite authors on Bookbub? If you subscribe to Bookbub — (and if you don't, why don't you? - They'll send you daily emails alerting you to sales and new releases on just the kind of books you like to read!) — follow me to make sure you don't miss the next Ginger Gold Mystery!

BB Follow on BookBub

a + Follow on Amazon

g follow me on goodreads

www.leestraussbooks.com
leestraussbooks@gmail.com